W9-AHK-298

I opened the door and stepped into a dimly lit, lavishly furnished room. In the center of the room stood Nell Virdon, totally and beautifully naked.

"I must be crazy," she said.

"Why?" I asked, walking over to her. "People who know what they want aren't crazy."

"Do you know what you want?" she asked, wetting her lips.

"I knew what I wanted as soon as I saw you," I told her.

"So did I," she said, putting her arms around my neck and drawing my mouth down on hers.

*Don't miss any of the lusty, hard-riding action in the
new Charter Western series, THE GUNSMITH:*

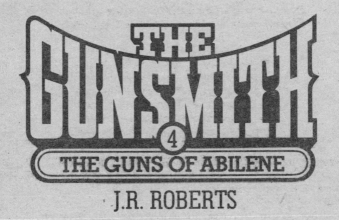

THE GUNSMITH

4

THE GUNS OF ABILENE

J.R. ROBERTS

ACE CHARTER BOOKS, NEW YORK

THE GUNSMITH #4: THE GUNS OF ABILENE
Copyright © 1982 by Robert J. Randisi
All rights reserved. No part of this book may be reproduced in any form or by
any means, except for the inclusion of brief quotations in a review, without
permission in writing from the publisher.

All characters in this book are fictitious. Any resemblance to actual persons,
living or dead, is purely coincidental.

An Ace Charter Original

ISBN: 0-441-30859-7

First Ace Charter Printing: April 1982
Second Printing: November 1982

Published simultaneously in Canada

Manufactured in the United States of America

Ace Books, 200 Madison Avenue, New York, New York 10016

To the Guns of Abilene:

Wild Bill Hickok
John Wesley Hardin
The James Brothers
Ben Thompson

Without them there would have been no story.

Prologue

In 1871, Abilene, Kansas wasn't exactly Sodom and Gomorrah, but it came pretty damned close. It was a wide-open cattle town with prostitutes, bushwackers and gamblers—especially gamblers—lining up to relieve the cowmen of their hard-earned money.

For a town as wild and tough as that, you needed a lawman just as tough. Up until 1870, two-fisted Tom Smith was the law in Abilene; and he indeed ruled with his fists, not with guns, until he was shot down. However, the law in Abilene in '71 not only lived by his guns, he knew that he'd eventually die by someone else's guns—as is the case with me, too.

His name was Wild Bill Hickok.

Mine's Clint Adams.

Bill's name was his calling card, because everybody knew who Wild Bill was. With me it was a little different. Through the years I had built up a reputation as both lawman and—for want of a better word—a gunman. Some years ago an overzealous newspaperman had christened me "The Gunsmith" because of my proficiency with guns—not only for shooting them, but for modifying and building them —and the name had stuck. So, while I am not exactly ashamed of them, I realize that the name and the rep are very likely to get me killed one day, and the same can be said for Bill.

I had heard that Bill was the law in Abilene, and would have gotten around to dropping in on him sooner or later, even if I hadn't spotted the ads he'd been placing in newspapers throughout the country.

I was in Texas when I first saw it. I'd just gotten out of a mess down Mexico way, and I'd had to kill a young gunfighter who thought I was his ticket to a reputation. Instead, I turned out to be his ticket to Boot Hill. I wasn't happy about that, and I was also depressed because of a mongrel dog who'd picked me up in Oklahoma and followed me all the way from Texas, saving my life a couple of times along the way. Seems that after that adventure was over, the dog decided it was time to go his own way, and damned if I didn't miss that big, red dog.

Anyway, the ad read like this:

> *Wanted: A Gunsmith, not for his ability to repair guns, but for his ability to use them. Apply: Abilene, Kansas*

Knowing the power of his reputation, Bill knew he didn't have to sign his name to the ad. It was common knowledge that he was now marshal of Abilene, and he knew his message would find its way to its intended recipient. Me.

1

Before noon, Abilene looked just like any other town. A little busier perhaps, but still kind of quiet and peaceful. I had already decided that when I rode in I'd look for a saloon first and Bill second.

There were easily a dozen saloons in Abilene, but I settled on the Bull's Head, one of the largest. It had a painting of a bull over the entrance, but it seemed that part of the bull had been painted over for some reason—the part identifying him as a male.

Gaming tables dominated the interior of the large saloon. Roulette, blackjack, dice, faro and poker tables were very much in evidence, and even at this time of the day, some of them were in use. Poker was virtually the only game I indulged in, but it was too early in the day for me—at least, too early in this day.

However, it wasn't too early for a drink, especially when you've just come off the trail with an inch of dust lining your throat.

"Beer," I told the bartender.

"Feel like a game, friend?" he asked as he set a mug of foam down in front of me.

"Like what?" I asked. "Find the beer in the foam? Bring me a beer, friend!"

He threw me a withering look, but did as I asked and brought a maximum of beer with a minimum of foam.

"Stop scarin' my barkeep, Adams," a voice said from just behind me and to my left.

I took a very deliberate drink from my beer before putting the mug down and turning my head to look at Ben Thompson. He was a tall, good-looking man of about twenty-eight. Once his temper had been deadly, but he'd learned to control it. Now his gun hand was deadly, and he killed with a total casualness that was awesome.

"Hello, Ben," I said. He was sharply dressed, looking more like a gambler than a gunman. "Give up your guns for a deck of cards?"

"Almost," he told me. He swept back his jacket to show me a four-shot Colt cloverleaf in a shoulder rig.

"Didn't know you favored shoulder rigs, Ben," I told him.

"Don't," he told me, letting his jacket close, "but my partner favors it over my carrying a .45 on my hip in this getup," he told me.

"Your partner?" I asked.

"Yeah, Phil Coe," he told me. "He and I own this place."

"Coe," I repeated. "Do I know him?"

"I don't think so. Phil's a gambler. This place was his idea, and he invited me to invest in it. If you're gonna be around town awhile you'll probably meet him. And if you're gonna do any gambling this is the place to do it."

I looked around the place again, then back at Thompson, and said, "I'm impressed, Ben. Going into business for yourself, huh?"

"Man's gotta do something else besides fire a gun,

Clint. Enjoy the beer, it's on the house."

I'd never known Ben Thompson to think of himself as anything but a gunman before, and I was impressed with the fact that he had a part interest in the Bull's Head Saloon—and with what he said about a man having to do something other than fire a gun.

I also wondered how he was getting along with Hickok, now that Bill was the law. Two gunfighters often reacted like two bulls when they're put in the ring together. I always got along with Bill, but not everyone did.

Thompson cornered the bartender and talked to him for a good minute straight, while the man just listened. I suspected he was telling the barkeep that my beer was on the house, and to stop serving foam instead of beer.

I'd never heard of this guy Phil Coe, but he'd gotten Ben Thompson to wear a suit and a pocket pistol, so he must have been a smooth talker—which most professional gamblers were.

I finished my beer and turned down another one, which the barkeep told me was also on the house.

"As long as Mr. Coe don't find out," he added.

"What's that mean?" I asked. "Ben Thompson said it was."

"Yeah, but Mr. Coe's the boss," the guy told me.

I looked at him and asked, "And what's Mr. Thompson?"

He shrugged. "Mr. Coe figured having Ben Thompson around would help to avoid trouble."

"I see," I said, and I did. Suddenly my opinion of Mr. Coe, whom I hadn't even met, hit rock bottom.

So Coe had asked Thompson to become a "partner," only so he'd have Ben's gun around to keep the peace. I wondered how Thompson would react if I tried to tell him that, or if I even had the right to butt in.

The Bull's Head suddenly wore thin on me, and I decided to go and find Hickok and see what his message was all about.

2

There were a couple of livery stables in town, and I put my rig up at the one closest to the Bull's Head. As was always the case, I gave the livery man some extra money to make sure he took proper care of my big black, Duke.

Also, as was always the case, he was impressed with Duke's size and stature.

After that I sought directions to the marshal's office, but when I got there the door was locked, which I found odd.

I stood on the boardwalk in front of the office, wondering where I'd find Bill. If he wasn't in his office, chances were good he was in one of the saloons, probably involved in a card game. I knew he wasn't in the Bull's Head, so I tried the only other saloon in town that equaled it in size, the Alamo.

I pushed through the glass front doors and was impressed by the setup I found inside. Every spare inch of room was taken up by a gaming table of one kind or another, and at the rear of the room, sitting with his back to the wall as always, was Bill Hickok, playing poker.

I noticed an empty beer mug to Bill's right, so I

went to the bar, ordered two beers, and carried them to the table.

I slapped it down on the table next to Bill without spilling a drop and said, "Can't be playing this game all dried out."

He was looking at the three cards he'd just drawn to two kings, and he'd pulled a third king and a pair of fours.

"Stand by," he said without looking up, but I knew that he was talking to me. "Your play," he told the opener.

I had no idea how many cards the man had drawn, but when he made his bet Bill promptly raised him when it came his turn. There were four other players and they all dropped out as a result of the raise. The opener looked at Bill across the table and then called.

"Kings full," Bill announced, and the other man threw his hand down in obvious disgust, because his cards landed face up, revealing an ace-high flush.

Bill raked in his chips and told the dealer, "Cash me in." Rising to his feet he said to the other players, "Thank you, gents." Then he turned to face me with his hand out.

"Hello, Clint. Glad you got my message."

"Couldn't very well miss it, Bill," I answered, taking his hand.

"New scar, huh?" he asked, touching his left cheek to indicate the scar I had on mine. It ran from below my eye to my jaw.

"Relatively."

Bill was an impressive figure of a man. He was good-looking, despite an oversized nose, and he had a long, flowing mustache and long hair which he kept neat and clean. On his hip he wore a Smith & Wesson .32, which was light and aided the fast draw—not that he needed help. It was as deadly as a .45 in the right hands, and his were the right hands.

He picked up the beer I'd brought him and said, "Let's sit down." I followed him to another corner table, and he sat with his back to the wall. I sat so I could see him and the front entrance of the saloon.

"Guess you're wondering why I called for you," he said.

"I'm a little curious about it, yeah," I admitted.

He drank half his beer, then put the mug down and settled back in his chair. "This is a rough town, Clint, as I'm sure you've heard tell," he began.

I nodded. "I've heard."

"Well, things are getting a little rougher these days. I suppose you saw the Bull's Head when you rode in."

"I not only saw it, I went in for a drink."

"Why?" he asked quickly, his eyes narrowing. And if I didn't know Bill better I would have said he was suspicious.

"I was thirsty," I said, staring right into his eyes, holding his gaze.

"Did you see Thompson?" he asked.

"I did. Bought me a drink," I answered. "Bill, you're not having trouble with Ben, are you?"

He made a face and replied, "Not so much Ben as his slick partner, Phil Coe."

"The gambler. Ben told me about him, and so did the bartender. My opinion is not high."

"Then it's right on the money," he told me. He grabbed his beer and finished it, signaled the bartender for two more. When the man brought them Bill said, "Put it on my tab, Ralph."

"Sure thing, Marshal."

"Coe is running crooked games over there, Clint. I

know it, but I can't prove it."

"That's not why you sent for me, is it?" I asked him. "I'm not a gambler, Bill."

"No, that's not it," he assured me. "There are other problems with Coe. Did you see that painting over the entrance to the Bull's Head?"

I thought back to the mutilated painting hanging over the entrance to the saloon, the bull with his private parts covered up.

"Seems to me it was painted over some," I told him.

"It was lewd and insulting to the womenfolk in this town," he told me. "I ordered him to paint over it, and he refused."

"But it was done."

"I had it done, and he's sworn he'll get me for it. He's been passing rumors that I've got it in for all Texans, and believe me, Clint, at any given time this town is chock-full of Texas cattle men. There's gonna be an explosion and that's where you come in."

"How?"

He nodded. "I need you to back me up, Clint. I need someone I can trust."

"How many deputies do you have, Bill?"

"One, and only because Mike Williams is a friend of mine. I can't get anyone else to stand with me."

"Is he good?"

"He's a friend, Clint, probably the only one I've got in town. He carries a shotgun, because he can't miss with that."

"I see."

What he was telling me was that it would be him and me and an inexperienced third man against Coe and whatever Texans he could incite to go against Bill Hickok.

"Aside from Coe, there's still plenty of trouble in this town," he added.

"Why not ask Thompson?" I asked him.

He shook his head. "Ben's been bamboozled by Coe's slick talk. Besides that, he's got a wife and kid and he's happy as a pig in shit running the Bull's Head."

"Only Coe's the real boss," I added.

"And Ben don't know it."

"Have you tried to tell him?"

"Ain't my affair, Clint, 'less'n I was thinkin' of askin' Ben to take up with me, which I ain't."

We both lowered the levels of our glasses some, and then he added, "But I'm askin' you."

Last time I'd seen Bill, he and a young feller name of Earp had stood with me against six hardcases, and we'd come out without a scratch. Without Bill's help, I might have caught my last bullet right there and then.

"You know I'll stand with you, Bill," I told him. "You knew it when you first placed those ads."

He smiled and said, "You're damned right I did!"

We had another couple of beers to seal the deal, and then Bill said, "You come over to my office later and I'll give you a star to wear."

I balked at that. "Why don't we play it low key, Bill," I told him. "No star. Let's keep my reasons for being in town a little quieter than that."

He glanced at me, wondering if there might be another reason why I didn't want to wear a star, but he didn't ask.

"Sounds like a good idea," he told me. "Let's do 'er that way."

It was getting on past noon now, and business at the tables was picking up. A few girls had shown up also, mingling with the customers, shilling at the tables and pushing drinks.

"I know who owns the Bull's Head," I told Bill, "but who owns this place?"

"Would you believe me if I told you that a woman owns the Alamo?" he asked.

"Really?" It wasn't such an unbelievable statement, but it was surprising.

"And a looker, too," he added. "Nell Virdon is her name. She should be out sometime this evening. Nell usually stays in during the day."

"She running girls?" I asked.

"You interested?"

"Just curious," I said, eyeing a redhead in a shimmering green gown who was working the faro table. She looked up and caught my eyes, held them momentarily, and then smiled and went back to her dealing.

"Didn't know you were a faro player," Bill commented, following my gaze.

"I'm not," I said, looking back at him. "Might find myself a poker game, though, later tonight."

"They run a nice game here," he said.

"Not here," I told him. "At the Bull's Head." I finished my beer and added, "Couldn't very well do that if I was wearing a star, could I?"

"You got a point there, partner, you got a point there."

3

I left Bill at the Alamo to return to his poker game. I wanted to get myself settled in a hotel and take a bath.

Bill had recommended the American House Hotel, the largest in Abilene. I was surprised when I entered the lobby to find that the desk clerk was a female. She was a young girl of about eighteen who was wearing a simple blue dress, but the body inside that dress was anything but simple. She had pert, rounded young breasts that jutted impudently at me from behind the desk. She had long, brown hair that had a clean, fresh scent, and wide, innocent-looking brown eyes.

"Well," I said, approaching the desk and putting my saddle bags down on the floor, "you certainly are the prettiest desk clerk I've ever seen."

She blushed and her eyes fell for a moment, then came back up and captured mine boldly.

"Thank you, sir," she said. "Would you like to sign in?"

She presented me with the registration log and I signed it and turned it around so she could read the name.

"Mr. Adams?"

"That's right, and what might your name be?"

"Althea," she said, shyly. "My friends call me Allie."

"Well, I hope we'll become friends," I told her sincerely. "So you won't mind if I call you Allie?"

"Not at all." She turned around to fetch a key, presenting me with a fine view of her delicately curved back, and full womanly hips.

When she turned back she caught me looking and blushed prettily again. "Your key," she said.

I brushed her hand deliberately as I took the key from her, and she tried to snatch it back to her without seeming to.

"Can I have someone show you to your room?" she asked.

I bit back a reply that might have embarrassed her, looked at the room number on my key, and said, "No, I'll be able to find it, thank you."

"We start serving dinner at five o'clock, Mr. Adams," she told me. "The food is very good here."

"I'm sure it is," I told her, "but I wouldn't even think of trying it unless you agreed to call me Clint."

"All right . . . Clint."

"I'd also like a bath," I told her.

She seemed about to blush again as she told me, "We have one on every floor, Mr.—I mean, Clint. With hot water available."

"Okay, Allie, thank you," I said, picking up my gear, "I think I'm going to enjoy my stay here in Abilene."

"I hope you do," she replied.

I smiled at her and then went upstairs in search of my room and that sorely needed bath.

After the bath I decided that I was too hungry to wait for dinner, so I went back downstairs to the lobby. I was disappointed to find that Allie had been replaced at her post by a foppish-looking man.

I approached the desk and asked, "Can I still get lunch in the dining room?"

"Why certainly, sir," he replied snobbishly. "We have the finest cuisine in all of—"

"Thanks," I told him, cutting him off. I walked into the dining room.

It was past lunch time for most, so the large, lavishly furnished dining room was almost empty. I sat down and ordered a steak from a tired-looking waitress who appeared to be just about dead on her feet.

"Is that all, sir?" she asked.

"That's it. Just a steak and a beer, please."

"Yes, sir."

Although her face was worn, she was in her early thirties, blonde, and had a nice, solid body. As I watched her walk back to the kitchen, I realized that I hadn't had a woman for nearly three weeks, and the itch was getting stronger.

When she came back with the steak, I noticed that she had deliciously round breasts and hips, and I was getting itchier by the minute.

"Thank you," I told her as she put the food down in front of me. In sharp contrast to young Allie, the waitress's hair smelled of fried foods, and her body smelled of perspiration; but if there was one odor in the world that failed to offend me, it was the smell of a woman's sweat. In this instance it had an instant effect on me and I had to squirm in my seat as a painful erection began to build. Her eyes met mine, and I wondered if she realized what was going on under the table.

"My pleasure, sir," she told me, holding my gaze.

Yeah, I thought, she knew.

I tried to ignore my condition and pay attention to my lunch, but I knew I'd have to do something about it tonight. For a man who enjoys women as much as I do, three weeks is an awful long time to go without one.

The steak was tender and juicy, and after a couple of bites it began to command all my attention. When she came back with my check, I paid it and added a generous tip.

"Come back if there's anything else we can do for you, sir," she told me.

"I will," I answered, "thank you."

"Thank *you*."

It was almost three when I left the hotel, and I decided to go over to the Bull's Head and sit in on a game.

When I entered the saloon, gambling was in full swing. The sound of raised voices, crying out in either defeat or victory, however momentary and fleeting, was deafening. The atmosphere here was a little more brazen than that of the Alamo, and the clientele more raucous. I sought out the poker tables with my eyes, and found them both filled. While waiting for an opening, I went to the bar for a drink.

"Beer," I told the bartender, the same one who had been on duty that morning. He stared at me until I put my hand in my pocket and came up with the price of the drink. As he went for the beer I called out: "And mind the foam!"

It must have caused him considerable pain, but he brought me a mug filled with foamless beer.

"Thanks," I said.

I turned my back to the bar and watched the poker tables as I drank it. I glanced idly around from time to time, looking for Ben Thompson, but he was no-where in sight.

I called the bartender over at one point and he came, although reluctantly. "Yeah?"

"Is Phil Coe around?"

His eyes flicked quickly around the room, and then he answered, "He's not out yet. Why?"

"Ben Thompson said he'd like me to meet his part-ner. I thought that since Ben wasn't around right now, I'd introduce myself. Guess I'll have to wait un-til later."

Just then a cowhand got up from one of the tables.

"Excuse me, there's my opening," I told the barkeep, and made for the empty chair.

I sat down and bought twenty dollars worth of chips from the dealer, a small man with thinning gray hair and quick hands. Remembering what Hickok had said about a crooked game, I paid more attention to the dealer's movements than I did to my own cards for the first few hands, and consequently I lost. I didn't however, notice the dealer doing anything he shouldn't, so I concentrated on my cards from there on in.

I took a few hands after that, and then after inspect-ing each player in turn and getting their habits down pat, I began to assume control of the game.

The best player among the cowhands at the table was the man directly across from me. He was about twenty-seven or so and his clothes were well-worn from travel. He played the game with great concen-tration, and he played well, but he had one idiosyn-crasy that I caught onto fairly early.

The game was seven-card stud and this fellow had a habit of placing his first two hole cards just under-neath his face cards *when he had a pair in the hole,* otherwise he would just drop the hole card down on the table casually. In every instance, however, when he placed the hole cards neatly together, with the tips beneath the face cards, he would end up having a pair. Thus, when a card fell face up and he raised on it, I'd know that he had three of a kind and I would either drop out or, if I knew I had him beat, double his raise.

Consequently, every time he took a hand, I would already have dropped out two or three cards before. I thought that after a while he began to notice this.

There was another man standing near the table, to this man's right, and the resemblance told me that they were brothers. They both had mustaches, but the standing man was at least three years older than the seated one.

On one hand, an ace of diamonds dropped on his hand as the fourth card, and he immediately raised. I had already noticed that he had his pair in the hole, and this meant that he had three aces. One of my hole cards was his fourth ace, so there was no danger of his having four aces at any point in the game.

My other hole card was a king of spades, which matched the suit of the ace I held.

On the table I had the ten of spades and the queen of spades. After four cards, I was lacking the jack for a straight flush to the ace.

He was showing the ace of diamonds, and a four of hearts. His fifth card was a four of clubs, and I knew he had aces full. His face reflected nothing, but all had seen him raise of the ace, and now he had a pair to boot. The other players dropped out on his bet, but I was ahead and played a hunch by calling. My fifth card had been no help, being a lowly trey, but I had two more coming. And I had noticed from ev-

eryone else's face cards—before they folded—that my
jack was still alive, and since he had two aces in the
hole, I knew he didn't have it.

My sixth card was another trey, giving me a useless
pair of them. His sixth card was a nine of spades, and
I felt a tingle in my hands, as if the jack would come
out on the heels of the nine—but would it come to
him, or to me?

We'd drawn a small crowd by then, and the dealer
dealt out the last hole card.

He looked at his and showed to emotion. I looked
at mine and felt like spitting on it. It was a jack, all
right, but a jack of hearts. I had my straight, but it
did not beat his full house.

All that remained was for me to bluff him out.

Most of the money on the table had been bet before
the two of us, so when he bet a hundred, I raised him
five hundred, which was half my winnings. He had
about six hundred dollars in chips left, and he pushed
them all forward.

"Call and raise," he said.

"Raise a hundred," the dealer called.

He had me, but after what I'd paid so far, a hundred wasn't too much to pay for a look at his last
card. I considered raising him again, which would
cause him to look for a stake somewhere, but decided
against it.

"I call."

He turned over his hole cards and I looked at them
in surprise. He had a pair of aces in the hole, all right,
but it was his third card that gave it to him. His original two hole cards had been an ace—and a five!

I had been right. He'd noticed me watching him
and knew that I had caught on to his habit when he
was holding a pair in the hole. He'd made me think

he had a pair in the hole, and with a larger final bet, would have caused me to drop out.

I turned over my hole cards, revealing my straight.

"Straight beats two pair," the dealer announced, and I raked in my chips.

My opponent shrugged and stood up. "I'm cleaned out," he said, looking at me.

"Sorry, friend," I replied.

"No problem," he told me. "I had a good ride for the twenty dollars I sat down with. You play a good game."

"So do you. Will you and your brother have a drink on me?" I asked.

I thought he might take it as an insult, but his brother said, "Jess," and that seemed to have a soothing effect on him.

"Thanks, friend," his brother said. "We'll take you up on that offer."

He put his hand on his brother's shoulder and they both made for the bar. The dealer looked up and made eye contact with the bartender, conveying the message that their drinks were on me.

The dealer leaned towards me and asked, "Do you know who those two are?" he asked.

I looked back at him and shrugged. "Brothers, from appearances, that's all I know," I told him.

"Brothers, sure," he said, "but the James brothers. Frank and Jesse. You just cleaned out Jesse James!"

4

Frank and Jesse James finished their free drink and left the Bull's Head. I stayed a while longer, playing evenly, and quit while I was almost two thousand dollars ahead. I hadn't seen any evidence of a crooked game, but then I spent all my time at one table with one dealer.

I cashed in my chips and went to the bar for a drink.

When the bartender brought me a beer he said, "You still want to meet the boss?"

I looked at him innocently and asked, "You mean Mr. Coe?"

He gave me a look that said "Who else?" and replied, "Yeah, Mr. Coe."

"Sure."

He walked to the other end of the bar and spoke to a well dressed man in his mid-thirties who was watching all of the activity in the room. The man leaned back to give the bartender his ear, then looked down the bar at me. He spoke to the bartender again, then started walking towards me.

"Mr. Coe?" I asked as he reached me.

He hesitated a moment to take a drink from the

bartender, then said, "That's right. I understand you're a friend of my partner's."

"Well, not a friend, actually. More like an acquaintance. My name's Adams, Clint Adams."

Coe stuck his hand out and as they shook said, "Adams—that name sounds familiar."

"Does it?" I asked, not offering him any help in remembering. Let him ask Ben Thompson about it.

"Nice place you have here, Mr. Coe," I complimented him.

He liked that. "Finest gambling house in town," he said, beaming. "Or even the state, for that matter."

"I was over at the Alamo earlier," I told him. "They seem to have a real nice place, too."

He frowned. "That may be, but it can't hold a candle to the Bull's Head. As soon as we get rid of Hickok, we'll be all set."

"Having trouble with the marshal?" I asked.

"Nothing that we can't handle. Hickok lost a bundle here one night, and since then he's been insisting that we run a crooked game here. You just played poker for a few hours, Mr. Adams, and you did quite nicely for yourself. Did you see any sign that a crooked game was being run?"

"No," I replied, "I can't say as I did."

"That's 'cause there wasn't any and most people know it. Still, we can't afford having Hickok going around spreading rumors."

"How do you plan on getting rid of him?" I asked. "He's the law, isn't he?"

"He won't be for much longer, I assure you," he said confidently.

I decided to dig at him a little and see how he reacted. "What happened to your painting out front?" I asked. "Seems to be part of a bull—"

"That was Hickok's doing, too," he said, his hatred of Bill showing plainly on his face.

"Can't you have it done over?" I asked.

"I intend to, after Hickok is—" He stopped himself short.

"After what?" I prodded.

"After he's gone," he amended. He hastily finished his drink and then said, "Enjoy your drink, Mr. Adams. It's on the house for a big winner like yourself."

"Well, thank you, Mr. Coe. This is a right friendly place."

"I'll be seeing you," he said, and walked off to oversee his empire.

I finished up my beer and slapped the mug down on the bar. The bartender looked over unhappily, but I turned around and walked out.

On my way back to the hotel I passed by an alley and became aware of some commotion going on. I wasn't a deputy, even unofficially, I was only in town to back Bill's play. But I decided to check it out anyway.

I walked into the alley cautiously and, as my eyes gradually adjusted to the darkness, I became aware of two men with a woman backed against the wall. One man had a hold of her breast and was squeezing it cruelly. The other man seemed to be groping around under her dress.

"Please . . ." I heard her saying.

"C'mon, honey, all we want's a little fun," one man was telling her.

"Please," she said, again. "I'm not—I'm not—" And then I heard her gasp in pain as the man holding her breast twisted it violently.

"Let her go!" I called out, and all activity froze momentarily.

Both men looked over at me, and then the larger

one, without removing his hand from beneath her dress, said, "Move on, friend, or we'll have our fun with you first."

"You're welcome to try, *friend*," I told him. "But I'd advise you to let go of the lady first." Then I added, "Unless you're planning on hiding behind her."

"Shit, Eli!" the man snapped to the other one. "Let's teach him."

"I'll gun 'im," the man named Eli began, but his friend cut him off. He flung the woman to the ground and said, "I don't need no gun for this dude." Then he started toward me.

I let him make the first move. As big as he was, with bulging arms, I figured he'd want to get those arms around me, so I waited for him to make his lunge. When he did I sidestepped him and hit him behind the left ear with my right. He slumped to his knees and I kicked him in the small of his back, driving him to the ground face first, all the air gone from his body.

I turned in time to find the second man reaching for his gun, and I knew right off that I didn't have to kill him—he was that slow.

I drew my gun in one swift motion and cocked it. He heard the sound that the hammer made and froze, staring down the barrel of my gun.

"Jesus!" he breathed.

"Do you want to die?" I asked him.

He shook his head quickly.

"Then pick up your friend and be on your way," I told him. "If I see either one of you in town tomorrow, you won't get off as easy."

He started nodding his head violently and went to help his friend up.

"Eli—" the other man began, but his friend cut him off.

"Shut up and walk, Homer," he told him, then practically dragged him from the alley.

I holstered my gun and went to help the woman to her feet. Once she was standing I recognized her as the waitress from the hotel.

"Well, we meet again," I told her.

Brushing herself off she said, "I don't know how to thank you."

"It's not necessary," I assured her. "But maybe I better walk you home, just to make sure you get there safely."

"Thank you," she said again.

We left the alley, and she led me to her room, which was on the second floor of a run-down, wood-framed building. The stairway was outside, and at the foot of it she said, "Well, thank you again, mister."

"I'll walk you up," I told her, and she looked at me a moment and then nodded.

When we got to the door she turned to look at me again and when our eyes met I knew we shared the same thought.

"Would you like to come in for a while?" she asked. Her eyes were shiny and slightly glazed, and I hoped it was from desire and not lack of sleep.

"I'd like that fine," I told her.

Her hair still smelled of fried foods, but I wanted a woman so bad that didn't matter.

Inside she lit the lamp and then turned to face me. I realized upon closer inspection that my original estimate of her age had been harsh, but then so had her life probably been. Looking at her now, she appeared to be in her late twenties. And if she hadn't looked so tired, she might even have been pretty. Her eyes were blue and her best feature by far—until you looked at her lush body.

"Are we thinking the same thing?" I asked.

"I think so," she said. "I ain't been thinking about nothing else since this afternoon."

I moved closer to her and put my hands on her shoulders.

"Mister," she said, "I ain't easy—"

"I know it," I told her. "Just relax."

I kissed her on the mouth, and for a moment she was stiff. But then her mouth opened and her tongue flicked into my mouth. Initially she even tasted like fried foods, but that quickly passed as pretty soon she just tasted like a girl—which was what I'd been needing for three weeks.

She broke the kiss and backed away, and I thought she was going to change her mind, but then she began to undress and I watched. Watching a woman undress was one of my favorite pastimes.

When she was naked she stood for my inspection. I was right about her breasts, they were large and round and firm, and pink-tipped. Her hips were full and her thighs were a bit meaty, but I didn't mind that. There was also a small roll of flesh around her waist, but I didn't mind that, either. The patch of hair between her legs was as golden as the hair on her head, but I knew that it would not smell like fried foods.

She watched then as I undressed, and her eyes went wide as she saw how ready I was. When I was naked she came eagerly into my arms and we fell to her bed together.

I kissed her mouth again, then her neck. I worked my way down to her breasts and began to nibble on her nipples. They started as little buds but quickly bloomed beneath my tongue. The day's sweat was still on her body and it tasted salty, but good. I licked all of the salt from both her breasts before continuing my downward course. When I reached the apex of her thighs, I found her wet and ready. I inserted two fingers into her and she began to grind her ample hips into the bed.

"Oh jeez, mister . . ." she gasped, the movement of her hips becoming more violent.

When my fingers were slick with her juices I moved to the little nub buried in her pubic hair, and it too bloomed. When I gave it a few swipes with my tongue, it swelled and then she erupted.

I was right. Her golden mound didn't smell like fried foods.

"Oh, mister, you've got me so hot!" she moaned.

I moved up beside her again and she grabbed my swollen member in her hands and began to stroke it.

"So hot. . ." she said again, sliding down until she could rub her nose against my tip. Her tongue flicked out, tentatively at first, but then more boldly, as it encircled the swollen tip. Then she opened her mouth and took me inside and, after three weeks, the sensation was almost more than I could bear. She might not have been easy, but she wasn't exactly inexperienced, either. Her cheeks hollowed out as she sucked on me and I enjoyed it. I had not found all that many women willing to do that sort of thing, and when I did I'd simply lay back and let them go as long as they wanted.

When she'd had enough—and me too, almost—she straddled my hips and reached behind her to guide my shaft to the lips of her nest. When she had me poised she raised her hips a little more, climbed aboard and then sank down on me, burying me to the hilt in her wet warmth.

"Oh, God!" she hissed. And she began to ride me

up and down with abandon. I reached up and put my arms around her, pulling her down flat on top of me. Then I reached around and cupped her buttocks and began to control the tempo myself. I had to slow her or it was all going to be over too soon.

"Oh yeah, yeah," she crooned with every slow stroke. I moved my fingers into her to spread her even wider, trying to get myself in deeper and deeper. She took all I could give her and begged for more.

I held her close and began to taste the new perspiration on her neck and shoulders.

"Over," I whispered in her ear. "Turn over."

Without breaking the fleshy link between us I turned her over and was now in complete control—or that's what I thought.

She had climaxed a few times already and her eyes appeared glazed over again. I was about ready and increased the tempo of my strokes. Her hands came around to grab my butt and pull me deeper, and her mouth opened but no sound came out. We were both sweating, and her large breasts were slick against my chest, the nipples like little pebbles digging into me.

"Oh . . . my . . . God!" she cried out as she felt me swelling inside of her, and then she screamed when I blew.

It had been a long three weeks.

5

The following morning I had breakfast at the American House, but my ladyfriend of the previous evening was not on duty that early. We had not exchanged names until I was ready to leave her room, and that's when I found out that her name was Sheila. We also agreed that what had happened had simply been something we both needed, and would probably not go beyond that one night.

After breakfast I went over to Bill's office, but once again I found it locked up. I found him at the Alamo, playing three-handed poker, without a house dealer. It appeared to be a private game.

He saw me when I walked in and acknowledged me with a wave of his finger. He called his hand, raked in his money, then said something to the two players and got up. He left his money on the table. When you're Bill Hickok you can do that and be sure it will still be there when you return.

The other men continued to play, two-handed.

"Aren't you ever in your office?" I asked.

He stiffened for a moment, then realized that I wasn't being critical of him.

"It's stuffy," he told me. "I can breathe better in here."

I wondered if Bill's dislike of the Bull's Head had anything to do with his obvious preference for the Alamo.

"Drink?" he asked. I frowned at him and shook my head.

"Too early," I said.

He got a shot glass of good whiskey from the bartender and tossed it down. I couldn't remember ever having seen him drink that early in the day.

"Bill, did you know that Frank and Jesse James were in town?" I asked him.

"Sure I did," he told me. "Those boys came to see me when they first got here. They told me they were just laying low for a while and not looking for any trouble, and I agreed not to breath down their necks."

"As long as you're sure," I told him.

"Of course I'm sure," he said. He called for another drink and tossed that one down, too.

"Seems like a lot of firepower for one town," I commented. I was thinking of Frank and Jesse James, Ben Thompson, Bill Hickok, and also myself.

"As long as we stay out of each other's way," he told me, "there shouldn't be any trouble. You leave those boys be, Clint."

"I don't intend to do otherwise."

"Good. I gotta get back to my game. How'd you do at the Bull's Head last night?"

"I won, and I couldn't see anything crooked," I said.

"It's a come-on, believe me," he said. "That was your first time there and they want you to go back. You'll see."

"Well, I'll go back tonight."

"You don't have to do that, you know. I just want

you here to back me up if something happens."

"I know, but I'm curious. I'll be back in here tonight, though. I want to meet the lady in charge."

"Yeah, you always did like your girl-flesh," he said, nudging my shoulder. "I expected to see you here last night, looking for some company."

"I did all right," I told him.

"Yeah, I 'spect you did."

Suddenly there was commotion at the front door, and a man came rushing through, almost slamming the doors open hard enough to break the glass.

"Rider coming into town, Marshal, thought you'd like to know about," the man said upon spotting Bill.

"Why's that?" Bill asked, seemingly uninterested.

"Well, I was down Texas way a while back and I recognize the kid."

"What kid?"

"Hardin, Marshal. It's Wes Hardin riding into town."

It seemed fated, somehow. With all of the firepower that was in town up until now, it seemed right that someone like John Wesley Hardin should ride in, too. Abilene was attracting all the best guns like a magnet.

"Hardin," Bill repeated, looking at me. "I've heard tell of him. He's just a kid, ain't he?" he asked me.

"Seventeen or so, I'd guess," I said, basing my estimate on what I'd heard.

"He's a killer, Marshal, pure and simple," the man told Bill.

"Well," Bill said, putting his empty glass on the bar, "I'd better see to him, then."

I wondered if Bill'd had any breakfast that morning. Those drinks he'd put down seemed to be effecting him more than they should. I decided to amble on out with him—unobtrusively.

Outside, the lone horseman headed straight for the Alamo, and as he approached I was struck at how young he really looked. He had to have been at least seventeen, but could have passed for less. When he dismounted and tied off his horse, I could see that he wasn't very big and didn't appear very dangerous. But then I looked at the two Colts strapped to his hips, tied down at the thigh, and I realized that he knew how to use them.

He stepped up on the boardwalk in front of the Alamo, and Bill stepped forward. As they faced one another, I leaned my back against the wall. I was just behind Hardin and could see Bill's face.

"Marshal," Hardin greeted. "Can I help you?"

"Name's Hickok, Hardin," Bill told him, "and I'll have to hold your guns while you're in town."

"My guns?" Hardin asked. I could see his head shaking as he said, "Nobody takes my guns, Marshal."

Bill's face froze, and I knew he'd interpret that as a challenge. "Son," he said to Hardin, "I'm *asking* you for your guns. I'd really hate to *take* them."

They faced each other for a few tense seconds while a small crowd grew, and then I saw Hardin's hands go down to his six-guns. He removed them from his holsters slowly and extended them to Bill butt first. As Bill reached up to take them, though, Hardin executed a perfect "road agent's spin," and Bill was looking down the barrels of John Wesley Hardin's guns.

"Still want my guns, Marshal?" the young killer asked.

I knew how fast Wild Bill Hickok was, but he wasn't fast enough to draw on Hardin in that situation. I also knew that this was exactly what Bill intended to do. He couldn't very well let Hardin back him down in front of the whole town. And I couldn't very well pull my gun and order Hardin to surrender his, because that would do Bill as much harm as backing down. I did the only thing I could do in that situation, aided by the tense silence that surrounded the situation.

I reached down, put my hand on the butt of my gun and cocked the hammer.

Hardin didn't flinch, but he'd heard it. I wasn't sure about Bill. His attention was solely on Hardin's face.

"Now, son, I don't want to have to kill you," Hickok said, which in the face of the situation as it stood seemed ludicrous. "So why don't we go inside, have a drink, and talk things over."

Hardin had to be taking the sound of my cocked hammer into consideration. Finally he made his decision. He lowered his guns, returned them to his holsters, and said to Bill, "All right, Marshal, that sounds like a sensible suggestion."

As they entered the Alamo together, I knew that, although the entire incident had taken scant minutes, people would be talking about the confrontation between Wild Bill Hickok and John Wesley Hardin for years to come.

I eased the hammer on my gun back down and followed them in.

6

The relationship between Hardin and Hickok changed drastically within a matter of minutes. There was a certain amount of hero worship in Hardin's eyes for Hickok, and Hickok seemed to take Hardin under his wing. One piece of advice he gave the young killer right off was, "Whenever you have a man under your gun, don't let him talk you out of it."

I never asked either man if they had heard my gun cock at that critical moment.

Hardin had ridden in with a trail herd from Texas, and I wondered if he knew Ben Thompson, who was also a Texan. I imagined that once Phil Coe heard that Hardin was in town he'd try and turn him against Hickok by telling him that Hickok hated Texans.

They had a few drinks together, and then Bill called me over and introduced us. Our eyes met, and I still couldn't tell if he had heard the hammer cock behind him, or if he knew it had been me.

"Adams," he repeated, much the way Phil Coe had when I introduced myself to him. "I've heard that name."

I gave him the same noncommittal answer I'd given

Coe, but Bill rushed in and gave Hardin a brief run-down of my activities over the years, and of our friendship.

"The Gunsmith," Hardin said. "Sure, I've heard of you." But there was none of the deep respect in his eyes for me that there was for Bill.

The reason for that, I think, was that in many parts of the country, Bill not only had a reputation as a gunfighter and a lawman, but as a killer. This was Hardin's reputation. I have been called many things in my time, but never a killer.

Bill was four years younger than me, and Hardin was about twenty years my junior, but both of their reputations were larger than mine—indeed, larger than life. There had been dime novels written about Bill Hickok, and I suspected there would be some written about Wes Hardin. But I did not think that such a fate was mine to look forward to. And I didn't much mind.

Upon closer inspection Hardin did look like a killer to me, and I took an instant dislike to him. I couldn't sit down and drink with him, so I made some excuse to Bill about still wanting to see the rest of Abilene. As I left the Alamo, they were joining the other two poker players.

The main street of Abilene, on which both the Bull's Head and the Alamo were located, was called Texas Street. I walked the length of it, taking in the other smaller saloons, the whorehouses, barber shops, general stores, while I considered the powder keg I was sitting on.

Thompson, Hardin, the James brothers, Hickok and myself. There was an explosion in there some-where, and Phil Coe might just turn out to be the detonator. As I often do when I want to think, I went to the livery stable to be with Duke.

"How you doing, big boy?" I asked him. He made noises at me, scolding me for having forgotten about him.

"I haven't forgotten you," I assured him, patting his massive neck. "It's this town—it's crazy. I think we're going to have to watch our step very carefully," I told him.

I wasn't even sure of Bill anymore. He wasn't the same man I remembered. He was drinking too much and there was something else about him that was bothering me, but I just couldn't put my finger on it.

I started to think about Hardin's arrival in Abilene. Was it coincidence—or had Coe, or his fellow Texan Thompson, sent for him?

Was he here to kill Bill Hickok? If he was, Bill was making it easy for him to do so: Ordinarily, Bill was a fine judge of character, but in this case he might be making the biggest—and the last—mistake of his life.

7

I decided to go over to the Bull's Head for want of something else to do. Maybe I'd find an early game of some kind, or maybe I'd sound Thompson out about Hardin. I didn't want to go back to the Alamo just yet.

When I reached the Bull's Head I stopped out front to take a closer look at their sign. It was obvious that it was originally a painting of a bull with an exaggerated sexual organ, and that part of it had been painted over. I could just see Bill standing out front, cradling a shotgun while the painters did the job. Not normally a prude, I wondered if Bill weren't really harassing Coe and Thompson for some private reason of his own.

When I entered the saloon my "friend" the bartender was not on duty, which pleased me. Although it was still early for me, I ordered a beer and figured to nurse it for a while. Foam seemed to be the house rule, but this time I didn't complain. When I turned, I saw Ben Thompson sitting at a table that I couldn't see from the door when I entered. I carried my beer over and asked him if I could join him.

"Suit yourself," he told me.

I sat down and saw that he was drinking coffee. He noticed me looking and said, "Would you rather have coffee than beer?"

"I think I would," I told him.

He nodded and raised a hand to the bartender, who brought me a cup of coffee and took away the beer.

"What's on your mind, Adams?" he asked.

"You know Wes Hardin?" I asked.

He looked at me, then said, "We've met, yeah."

"He rode into town this morning."

"Is that a fact?"

"Had a set-to with Bill Hickok right off the bat."

He looked interested at that. "Kill him?"

"No. Hickok tried to take his guns, then they decided to have a drink and talk it over."

"At the Alamo?"

"Yes."

He looked thoughtful.

"Ben, did you send for Hardin?" I asked.

"What, to kill Hickok?" he asked.

"Yes."

He shook his head, then said, "No, but it's not a bad idea."

"Hickok said he wasn't having too much trouble with you," I told him.

"We've been keeping clear of each other, but Phil's my partner. If he's having trouble with Phil, he's having trouble with me."

I stared at him hard for a moment, then asked him, "Ben, could you take Bill?"

His eyes bored into mine while he considered the question. "I can take anybody," he told me finally, and it sounded like a challenge—or it would have, had I chosen to take it that way.

"Do you have any intentions of trying him?"

He shook his head. "Hickok's a lawman. I'm not about to draw down on a lawman. If he didn't have that star. . ." he said, and left it hanging there.

"Would Coe have sent for Hardin?" I asked.

"Not without telling me," he said, which wasn't an answer. Before I could ask for clarification of that remark he asked me, "Are you here to back Hickok, Clint?"

"If need be, I'll back him." Which likewise was not a direct answer to his question.

"I hope it doesn't come to that," he said. "But Bill's been pushing us pretty hard."

"Why?"

"He lost a bundle in here one night. It was a blow to his pride. Or maybe he just doesn't like Texans; or maybe it's because the Alamo's his favorite watering hole."

"In other words, you don't know for sure."

"How could I, I'm not inside of the man's head," he replied irritably.

I drank some coffee while he stared into his. What he had said about being able to take anyone might just have been true. Ben Thompson was the best hand I had ever seen with a gun, with the possible exception of Wild Bill. I would not have liked to place a large bet on the outcome of such a facedown.

I finished the coffee and stood up. "Thanks for the coffee, Ben. Give my respects to your wife and son, will you?"

He looked up at me and said, "Thank you, I will, Clint. I'm taking them for a wagon ride this afternoon."

I left the Bull's Head, hoping I would not have to side with Hickok against Ben Thompson.

*   *   *

But the matter of facing Ben Thompson took care of itself that afternoon.

While taking his wife and child for a ride, his wagon hit a chuckhole, lost a wheel and threw the three of them. His wife suffered a broken arm, and Ben a badly fractured leg. Their young son emerged with a broken foot. Thompson would be laid up by the injury indefinitely.

So, Ben Thompson was no longer a factor in the impending explosion that would change the face of Abilene, Kansas.

8

That evening, for the first time since my arrival in town, I found Wild Bill in his office.

"I suppose you've heard Ben Thompson's out of action," I said to him.

"I've heard. How bad is his injury?"

"His leg is fractured and he'll be laid up for a long time. His wife may lose her arm."

"I'm sorry," he said sincerely. "And the boy?"

"He's young, he'll heal."

"That's good."

"Perhaps Coe will back off now," I told him, "without Thompson's gun to back him up."

"Perhaps," he agreed.

"Of course, there are other men in town whose aid he could enlist." I then added, "Other Texans."

He gave me a long, hard look and said, "You're speakin' of young Hardin."

"Yes, Bill. The boy's a killer, pure and simple."

"I'll remind you that some people say the same of me."

"We know better," I replied.

"Do we?" he asked. "Sometimes I wonder. You've killed enough men in your day, Clint," he reminded me, as if I needed to be reminded of such things.

"Never in cold blood, Bill."

"And I have?"

"Hardin has."

"Or so you've heard," he said. "Do you believe all the stories you've heard about me?"

"You've started most of them yourself," I noted, sidestepping the issue.

"That's true," he admitted. "I like young Hardin, Clint. I think I shall take him under my wing and keep him from going wrong."

I decided to avoid discussing the issue of how wrong John Wesley Hardin had already gone.

"Bill, did it ever occur to you that with Hardin being a Texan, perhaps Coe sent for him?"

"Did you question Coe?" he asked.

"I talked to Ben Thompson."

"And?"

"He said that he hadn't sent for him, and implied that Coe hadn't. He did, however, admit to knowing him."

"Not surprising, since both are from Texas and both have formidable reputations," he pointed out.

"I would keep my eye on Hardin, Bill."

"You keep an eye on Hardin," he told me, "and I'll keep an eye on the rest of the town."

"I wish you had more deputies," I told him.

"I made you the offer," he countered.

"I can do more good without the star."

"Well, then, I do have one additional deputy. His name is Tom Carson. He is a fair hand with a gun, and he signed on today."

That was hardly what I had in mind—one more man—but I said, "That's good. What about the James boys?"

"They pose no threat," he said confidently.

He looked at his watch and announced, "If you wish to meet Nell Virdon, now is the time."

He rose and once again I was struck at what a strikingly handsome figure he posed—with his low-crowned, wide black hat, his frock coat, his gun and bowie knife, his long hair and finely featured face. I knew that beneath that coat he had at least two hideaway guns, and as we were about to leave he picked up a rifle and cradled it in his arms. I knew about the hideaways because I had given him one of them, a two-shot .41-caliber derringer—a remarkably inaccurate gun in anyone's hands but his.

I followed him to the Alamo, which now, after dark, was in full swing. When we entered he stood a moment just inside the doorway, his eyes taking everything in before deciding it was all right to enter.

"There's Nell," he told me, and I looked over at the woman he was speaking of.

The mere sight of her made me catch my breath.

She was tall, about five-nine, with large, round breasts, a slim waist, and long legs. Her dark hair was piled up on top of her head, and her face was touched with just enough makeup to enhance her high cheekbones and generous mouth.

"Come on," Bill told me, "I'll introduce you."

I followed him across the room to where she was talking to three men, each of whom was trying to win her favor, and none of whom deserved it.

"Nell," Bill broke in, without so much as an "excuse me." The men all turned to see who was doing the interrupting, and when they saw Bill they all sort of melted away.

Nell Virdon turned to face us, and I caught the full impact of her up close. Unlike most women who are found in places like the Alamo, she did not drown herself in perfume, but just wore enough to make you want to lean closer to catch the scent.

"Good evening, Marshal," she greeted him, but she was looking at me.

"Nell, this is my good friend Clint Adams. He'll be staying on in Abilene for a while."

"I'm pleased to meet you, Mr. Adams," she said in a husky voice. She extended her hand to me as a man would and we shook.

"Welcome to Abilene," she added. "I hope we can do something to make your stay a little more pleasant."

"You already have," I told her, and she smiled at the compliment.

She turned to the bartender and told him, "Please give the marshal and Mr. Adams a drink on the house, Roy."

"Appreciate it, Nell," Bill told her.

"Thank you," I added, "but I'm afraid I became intoxicated the moment I laid eyes on you, Miss Nell. One more might be my undoing."

"Your friend is very gallant, Marshal," she told Bill. She then turned to me and added, "But I don't think one drink more will effect your presence of mind, Mr. Adams. You look like a man who can control his vices, whatever they are."

I told the bartender to bring me a beer, and Bill ordered the same. When they came Bill grabbed his and said, "If you two will excuse me, I think I will play a little poker."

"Please do. We could use a small donation from you."

"Tonight just might be the night I break the bank, Nell," he told her. "And then I'll own the Alamo, and you'll work for me."

"I wish you luck, Marshal," she said.

Bill went to one of the tables and made the players move so he could sit with his back to the wall. I took up my beer and stood next to Nell, leaning against the bar.

"This is quite a place you have here, Miss Nell."

"Just Nell, please . . . Clint. Friends should not stand on ceremony, don't you agree?"

"Does that mean that you and Bill aren't friends?" I asked.

"You mean because I address him as 'Marshal'? He's the law, and I address him with the respect due his position." She turned and picked up a drink I hadn't seen her order. "If, however, by that question you meant to inquire if the marshal and I were . . . 'friends,' the answer is no."

She'd caught the implication in my question, and I was pleased with the answer. I had every intention of bedding this gorgeous woman, and would have done so even if she and Bill were involved. But I was pleased that they were not.

"Have you sampled any of our wares, Clint?" she asked.

"I haven't done any gambling," I told her. "If, however, you mean have I been upstairs with any of your girls, the answer is likewise no." I looked into her eyes and added, "I do not believe in settling for second best when the best is available."

"The best is never simply for the asking," she was quick to point out, and I was tiring of the game.

"Miss Nell," I told her, "sometimes it is the best which has to *do* the asking. If you'll excuse me, I think I'll give the marshal some moral support."

I walked away and left her there speechless—but apparently not angry.

I walked to Bill's table and stood to his left. He

looked up and, since it was between hands, he asked, "And how are you and Nell getting along?"

"Fine, Bill," I told him. "It shouldn't be too long now," I predicted.

"Ha! Many have tried, old son."

"Yes, but I have a new approach," I told him. He gave me a puzzled look and I added, "I'm not going to try."

At that moment three hardcases came walking into the saloon and bulled their way to the bar, shoving aside several startled cowhands who, after seeing the size of the men who pushed them, decided not to push back.

I looked at Bill to see if he noticed, but he was squinting intently at his cards. On the heels of the three hardcases came a man with a badge. It was either Mike Williams or Tom Carson. Since I hadn't met either one yet, I didn't know which one.

The man with the badge came over to Bill. He leaned over to speak so only Hickok could hear him.

When the man straightened up, Bill said, "Mike Williams, meet Clint Adams. I've told you about him."

Williams, a big, husky fellow who wore no sidearm but carried a shotgun, nodded to me and then walked to the other end of the room.

"Gentlemen," Bill said after the hand, "duty calls. With a little luck, I shall return presently."

Bill walked to where the three hardcases were standing at the bar, laughing and shouting for service. I went across the room, so that Williams was covering Bill from one side, and I was on the other.

"Excuse me, gentlemen," Bill called out.

One of them turned at the sound of his voice, then nudged the others. Together they faced Bill. He'd left his rifle back at the poker table, and his hand as relaxed at his side. But I knew how quickly that hand could draw his .32 from its holster.

The hardcases obviously knew who he was, and at least two of them seemed unimpressed. The third seemed a little uneasy, but he had to stand with his friends. They were all roughly the same size, tall and broad, with the look of buffalo hunters.

They had another look, too. Every so often you see a man whose lust for a reputation prevents him from fearing anyone else, even Wild Bill Hickok.

The one in the middle had that look, and the other two would stand by him.

"Well, lookee here what we got," he said to his friends. "A long-haired marshal. Hello, Marshal."

"I'll have to ask you gentlemen to give up your guns," Bill told them.

"Why's that, Marshal?" the one in the center asked.

"I understand you've started a little ruckus at one or two of the smaller saloons in town," Bill told him. "We won't have anything like that happening here at the Alamo. Besides that, the law here in Abilene says that you have to surrender your guns when you enter town."

Two of the men wore theirs high, obviously not as fast-draw artists. The man in the center wore his low, and the way he was facing Bill, he obviously fancied himself able to use it. Bill would concentrate on him, ignoring the other two. I was hoping Williams wouldn't let go in the crowded room with that scattergun.

The spokesman looked around and then said, "Well, Marshal, I see a few men here still wearing their guns."

"Yeah, but I'm the law," Bill told him, "and I say you have to give yours up."

The man sucked in his wind, pushing his chest out, and told Bill Hickok, "Why don't you take it from me, Marshal."

Bill backed off a few steps. People began to scatter, looking for someplace to hide, but there were too many of them.

"Everybody stand still!" Bill shouted as loud as he could, with immediate effect. Everybody stopped moving and watched Bill anxiously.

"Mike," Bill said, speaking to Williams, "don't let loose with that scattergun. It's too crowded in here."

I saw Williams nod, but he did not lower the shotgun.

"You two men," Bill said now, speaking to the men on either side of the leader, "stand away from your friend. If he's in a hurry to die, there's no reason why you should join him. I'm giving you men a chance to save your lives."

The men looked at Bill, then at their loud-mouthed friend, and then at each other.

"Don't let him bluff you. His deputy can't use that shotgun because of the crowd. He can't outdraw all three of us. And I don't see anymore deputies."

The men looked around to see if their friend was right, and didn't see any other badges. It was time for me to speak up.

"Excuse me," I called out, and all three of them looked over at me. "I'm not a deputy, but if either of you men make a move for your guns, I'll kill the both of you."

The two men looked around the room, first at Bill, at each other, at me, and then back to Bill again.

"He's a volunteer," Bill told them. "He does it because he likes it. Now, step away from your friend.

He's about to make a big name for himself."

They stepped away from the other man, moving in opposite directions.

"The same way, please!" I called out.

It took them a moment to decide which way to go, but they finally got together on it and moved closer to me.

"Okay, mister," Bill told the loudmouth, "it's your move."

."You don't scare me none," the man sneered. "And you don't impress me, neither."

"Now that's a shame," Bill told him, "because I hope I'm very impressed with the man who finally kills me. But somehow, I don't think you're him."

It was deadly quiet in the room and I took a second to look for Nell Virdon. She was standing at the end of the bar, watching with interested eyes. She didn't look the least bit frightened, and if anything looked even more beautiful than before.

"Well, c'mon, big man," Bill prodded him, "you gonna draw or are we gonna stand here and see who dies a natural death first?"

The man's eyes flicked around the room, and that's when I knew he wasn't going to draw. That's the give-away, even before he starts to lick his lips and wiggle his fingers.

"Maybe the man would like to admit he made a mistake and ride out of town, Marshal," I suggested.

"You think so?" Bill asked without looking over at me. "What do you say to that, mister?"

Now the man licked his lips nervously and began to wiggle his fingers.

Finally he said, "I guess I made a mistake, Marshal."

"And?"

"And I'll ride out of town."

"Guess you were right, Clint," Bill told me. To the big man he said, "Unbuckle your gunbelt and put it on the bar."

When he had done so, I told his friends to do the same thing. Roy the bartender gathered up the hardware, and Bill told him, "Add that to your collection, Roy."

"Right, Marshal."

"All right, gents, you've worn out your welcome in Abilene. Get on your horses and ride," Bill told the three of them.

They shuffled out the door with their bodies half-turned, as if they were afraid they'd be shot in the back. Once they got outside, the sound of their footsteps on the boardwalk made it plain that they were trying to get far away from the Alamo—and Abilene—as quickly as possible.

Bill made a motion to Williams, who took his shotgun and went out the front door behind them.

"Okay, folks, let's get back to the business of losing money," Bill announced.

He turned to face me and I walked up to him. "You think Phil Coe sent them?" I asked.

He shrugged. "We'll probably never know. Thanks for the back up, Clint."

"That's what I'm here for, isn't it?"

Before he could comment Nell walked over. "Thanks for keeping my walls clean of bullets, Marshal," she told him. Then she turned to me and added, "You too, Clint. I appreciate a man who knows when not to shoot."

"I'd always prefer not shooting, Nell," I told her.

"That just might make you a minority," she told me. "Most men think it's more masculine to shoot."

"I've never had to justify my masculinity, Nell."

"If you people are gonna play word games," Bill broke in, "I'm gonna play cards."

He went back to the table and resumed his place, his back against the wall.

"He's right," I told her. "I don't like word games."

"No," she agreed, "neither do I." She looked around at the action, then said, "I guess Roy can handle things down here." She leaned over the bar and called Roy over. "I'll be upstairs for a while, Roy. Keep an eye on things."

"Sure, Miss Nell."

She said to me: "My room is the first door on the left, top of the stairs. Give me five minutes, okay?"

"Five minutes," I told her. "And not a second more."

9

Three hundred seconds later I knocked on her door.

"C'mon in," she called out.

I opened the door and stepped into a dimly lit, lavishly furnished room. In the center of the room stood Nell Virdon, totally and beautifully naked.

"I must be crazy," she said.

"Why?" I asked, walking up to her. "People who know what they want aren't crazy."

"Do you know what you want?" she asked, wetting her lips.

"I knew what I wanted as soon as I first saw you," I told her.

"So did I," she said. She closed the remaining distance between us, put her arms around my neck, and drew my mouth down to hers—although with her height I didn't have all that far to bend.

After a long, hungry, searching kiss she said, "No word games, Clint. I like to do . . . different things, different ways—"

"How about we invent some new ones?" I asked her.

She smiled and said, "Carry me."

I lifted her off the floor and walked with her to the

bed. I laid her on it, and she rose to her knees and began to undress me. No sooner were my pants around my ankles than she started using her mouth on me—her mouth, her tongue, her teeth, her hands. Hell, she even did things with her long hair, which hung down around her shoulders now.

After some time, she lay back on the bed and stretched herself luxuriantly. Several times she'd had me on the verge of exploding and had used her hands to prevent it. My legs were weak from the long session, and I stretched out beside her and began running my hands over her.

"Anything, Clint," she told me. "Do anything you've ever wanted to do with a woman."

Now that was a liberal attitude I had never run into with a woman before.

I began to run my mouth over her body, from her lips to her neck to her large breasts and brown nipples. As I continued to work my lips lower, I reached up and began to massage her breasts roughly. I squeezed them and tweaked her nipples until she was moaning with pleasure and writhing on the bed. When I was crouched between her legs I brought my hands down and spread them out further. Then I used my fingers to probe her and manipulate her until she was soaking wet. The scent of her began to work on my head, having a dizzying effect.

"Oh, Clint . . ." she moaned as I worked her into a frenzy with my fingers. When she seemed unable to take any more, I lowered my head and began to use my mouth and my tongue. She tasted salty, and I worked her love button with my tongue until it was as stiff and hard as it could be. When she was ready to go she grabbed my head and pulled it against her, grinding herself against my face.

"Oh yes, oh yes!" she cried over and over until the waves of pleasure she felt began to subside and gradually become feelings of pain.

But the pain seemed to excite her even more, and she bounced her buttocks off the bed, lifting me at the same time, showing more strength than I'd ever seen in a woman before.

When her nub became stiff again, I began to suck on it until she was almost screaming, her face buried in the pillow, her heels drumming against my ass.

"Oh, Lord. . ." she whispered when I finally stopped.

I moved myself up over her and sank myself deep inside of her. Her legs came up and wrapped themselves around my back and we immediately found the right tempo with no difficulty.

Her breath was coming in sharp gasps right in my ear, and the gasps became rasps and finally grunts. She climaxed again and I withdrew before I could follow.

"What—" she began.

"Turn over," I told her. I remembered how Sheila had enjoyed it that way.

"Over?" she asked weakly.

"You set the rules, Nell. Anything I ever wanted to do with a woman. So turn over."

I turned her over roughly and got her into position to receive me from behind. My erection was already sufficiently slick from her and when I spread the cheeks of her buttocks and told her, "Try to relax," entry came easily.

It was tighter, tighter than any woman had ever been. It took a few strokes this time, but then we found the tempo and my balls began to make slapping noises against her behind.

"You're . . . splitting me . . . apart!" she gasped, but that didn't stop her from matching me stroke for stroke.

When I finally came I felt as if I was shooting enough liquid to fill her up from head to toe.

"It's so hot!" she hissed.

My hands were gripping her breasts tightly, and when I withdrew and she turned over I could see that I'd left the imprint of my fingers on her fair skin.

"Did I hurt you?" I asked her.

She stretched her hands up over her head, causing her breasts to rise straight up, and sighed, "Oh, yes!"

10

I left her lying exhausted, face down in her bed, with one hand dangling to the floor. I covered her with a sheet so she wouldn't catch a chill, and then went back downstairs.

I went to the bar and told the barkeep, "Give me a shot, Roy."

He brought it to me, then leaned his elbows on the bar and said, "I gotta hand it to you."

"For what?"

"You're the first one who ever made it up there with her on the first night."

"Oh, yeah?" I asked, finding his remark funny. I tossed down my drink, enjoying the warming sensation it made going down. I said, "But not the first one to make it up there, right?"

"That's true," he told me. "There have been others who have gone up eventually, but you're the first to ever make it back down here first."

"Give me another one, will you?" I asked him, not quite sure what he meant.

"Sure!"

When he brought it I asked, "Any trouble?"

"No. The marshal's been cleaning up at poker and everything's been quiet." I finished the second drink and put the glass down.

"Well, I think I'll go over to the Bull's Head and see how things are over there."

"That's a nice place," he said, taking the empty glass away. "I used to work there."

That was very interesting. "Really?"

"Yeah, but that was some time ago."

"What happened?"

"I got fired."

"And that was a good recommendation for this job," I commented.

"Yeah, the best," he agreed, laughing.

This time I leaned my elbows on the bar to ask a question. "What do you know about Coe running crooked games?" I asked.

He thought a moment, then shrugged. I had the feeling that he'd made a decision some time ago about answering that question, if it ever arose. "I was never involved with the games, Mr. Adams," he said. "Just pouring the drinks."

"Was the marshal satisfied with that answer when he asked you the same question?" I asked him.

"He didn't push me on it," he told me.

I decided to play it the same way, for now. "All right, Roy. Thanks for the drinks. How much do I owe you?"

"No charge, Mr. Adams. You are now a preferred customer."

"Okay, thanks. I'll see you later."

When I went out into the darkness, I thought I saw a shadow across the street. As my eyes adjusted to the dimness, I could see that it was Mike Williams, Bill's friend and deputy. I waved at him and he returned the greeting.

I started off down Texas Street to the Bull's Head, wondering where Bill had Tom Carson stationed. It also struck me that I didn't know what Carson looked like, and he didn't know me, either. I hoped that wouldn't become a problem between now and whenever I finally met him.

I was halfway between the Alamo and the Bull's Head, out of sight of Mike Williams, when the first shot was fired. I started moving just before the second shot came or I'd probably be dead. It was a well-aimed shot, and only the fact that I was moving kept it from hitting me in the head. Even as I was rolling, I had the impression that each shot was fired by a different person.

From the direction of the Alamo I heard someone shouting, probably Williams. When I stopped rolling two slugs chewed up the boardwalk right in front of me. My gun was out and I was trying to locate something to shoot at when Williams came running up.

"Get down!" I shouted at him.

I'll give him this, his reflexes were good. No sooner had I shouted than he was rolling to his right. A couple of puffs of dirt appeared where he had been standing. Williams bounded back to his feet and made it into a doorway.

"Any idea where the shots are coming from?" he asked me.

"Across the street somewhere," I told him. "Up high, I think."

I looked up just as another shot was fired. Sure enough, I saw a flash from the roof of the general store.

"Did you see it?" he called.

"Yeah."

If he had a pistol or a rifle, I would have told him to cover me while I ran across, but at that distance the shotgun wouldn't be very effective.

"Mike, one of us has got to get across," I told him.

"Cover me," he called out, and took off.

I began to fire rapidly towards the roof and he made it across without being fired at. He signaled that he was safe, and I waved back and began to reload.

I fired at the roof again while Mike worked his way to the side of the store, where there were stairs going up to the second floor. From there he could get to the roof. Somehow, though, I had to get across to help him.

I backed into a doorway, hoping that I would be totally hidden from the snipers. I hoped they would assume that I was either working my way left, or right. I gave them a few seconds to decide, then took off directly across the street. It must have startled them, because they didn't begin firing until I was halfway across, and by then the shots were one step behind me.

Once I got to the other side they couldn't fire at me any more, so I rushed around to the side of the building where Mike had gone. When I got to the stairs I heard shots from the roof and took the steps two at a time. When I reached the top, I stood on the wooden railing and hiked myself up and over.

I'd had to holster my gun to pull myself onto the roof, and once I was up there I pulled it out again.

Mike Williams was standing between two men, one toward the front of the roof and one nearer the back. He had his shotgun trained on the man in the front, while both men had him covered with their guns. They were all deciding who was going to shoot who first and I made the decision for them. I fired at the man at the rear of the roof, catching him in the chest. He staggered back a few steps, fired an aimless shot into the air, and then fell to the roof floor. Mike didn't waste any time looking around, he fired both barrels at the other man, who was lifted and thrown off the roof by the force of the blast. When he landed in the street he was just so many pounds of chewed-up meat.

11

Neither man was familiar to Mike Williams or to me. They were dressed as trail hands, and their guns were in such condition that you knew they weren't professional shootists. Just a couple of cow hands who hired out as bushwhackers and couldn't do the job.

From the direction of the Bull's Head a man came running, carrying a shotgun and wearing a sidearm.

"Clint, this is Tom Carson," Mike said.

"You hear the shots, Tom?" I asked, wondering why he was coming along late.

"Heard one," he told me, "probably the last one. Sounded like a shotgun blast. Heard it just as I stepped out of the saloon," he explained.

"You know this feller?" I asked.

He leaned over to take a look at what the shotgun blast had left, then shook his head and said, "No, not from what I can see. Ain't much left of him, though. Give him both barrels did you, Mike?"

Mike nodded. He had a bloody tear in the left arm of his shirt where a single shot had scratched him.

"Take a look at the one on the roof, Tom, when you get a chance," I told Carson. "See if you know him."

"Sure."

"Mike, you better get somebody to clean up this mess."

"Right. I'll get the undertaker and some men. You gonna let the marshal know about this, Clint?" he asked.

"Later, maybe. All the noise in the Alamo, he probably didn't hear a thing. I don't want to distract him from his card game just yet. I'll tell him later."

Carson and Williams exchanged glances, then shrugged. Carson went around the building to make his way to the roof and see if he could identify the body up there.

"Drag him to the front and dump him off, Tom!" I called out. "He won't mind." I looked at Williams and said, "It'll make cleaning up a lot easier if they're both out here."

He shrugged again, not making a comment. "Where you gonna go now?" he asked me.

"Well, somebody hired these two jaspars to bushwhack me," I told him, "which means that somebody thinks I'm dead. I'm going to take a stroll over to the Alamo and see how people react when I walk in, alive and kicking."

"You want some help?" he asked, breaking his shotgun open and sliding two fresh shells in.

"No, Mike, you get this mess cleaned up. I'll be able to handle anything that comes up," I assured him.

"Suit yourself."

"I'll check in with you later."

"Keep your head down," he advised.

I waved and headed for the Alamo. There might be some surprised faces when I walked in, especially Phil Coe's, but I didn't think anyone would start blasting away when they saw me.

I wondered how many times Coe would have someone try to bushwhack me before hiring someone to call me out—that is, assuming Coe was behind the first attempt. Maybe I was doing him an injustice, but I didn't think so. There was no one else in town with any reason to have me killed. Ben Thompson must have told Coe—innocently or not—that I was here to back Wild Bill. And that wouldn't sit too well with the gambler.

I stopped before the doors of the Bull's Head, took a deep breath, and walked through. My eyes immediately sought Phil Coe, and found him standing at the bar, surveying the room. Gradually his eyes worked their way around until they fell on me. I thought I caught a slight jerk or stiffening of his back, but he covered up very quickly and simply nodded in my direction.

I continued to look around the room, wondering if Coe had imported a gunman yet, as I figured him to do with Ben Thompson out of action. I didn't see any familiar faces until my eyes fell on one of the poker tables. There, sitting with his back to the wall with his eyes on me was John Wesley Hardin.

12

I held the young killer's eyes until he dropped his gaze, to look at his cards. If he was so chummy with Hickok now, I wondered what the hell he was doing in the Bull's Head instead of the Alamo. Again I had to wonder if Phil Coe hadn't sent for Wes Hardin. The kid could very easily have signed on with a trail crew just so it would look like that was the only reason he'd ridden into Abilene.

I guess it remained to be seen if Hardin would eventually call one of us out—and I had the feeling that if he did call one of us, it would be me.

I went to the bar and ordered a beer. The bartender brought me foam. I guess he figured with Ben Thompson laid up he could go back to his old practices. Since I'd only ordered the drink as something to do, I let it go. The bartender seemed to consider that some kind of a victory over me and I didn't see any harm in allowing a small man a small victory.

Coe sidled over and said, "A little commotion down the street I understand, Mr. Adams. Would you know anything about that?"

"Not a thing," I told him innocently. "Quiet as a church out there when I walked in."

"I see," Coe said slowly. "I guess I must have been misinformed."

"I guess you were."

I drank some of my foam and said, "I see you have a young celebrity in the place tonight."

"Oh, you mean young Wesley?" he asked. "He's a Texan, you know, and as such he is welcome here. Ben and I both made his acquaintance some time back—in Texas, as a matter of fact. Yes, we are all very good friends."

"That's interesting," I told him. "It seems to me that he and Wild Bill got along very well when they first met."

"So I understand," he replied sourly. "I've spoken to the boy about being careful who he makes friends with, but of course the young must make their own decisions."

"I guess so."

"Seems to me you should also be careful about who you associate with, Mr. Adams. The marshal doesn't have that many friends in this town."

"Is that a warning, or a threat?" I asked.

"Oh, neither one, I assure you. It was simply a comment. I understand that even the town council is becoming disenchanted with his antics."

"Antics?"

"Drinking, gambling, not to mention his constant harassment of Texans. If he continues those actions, he could kill this town. Texans come in here with plenty of money to spend, Mr. Adams. The town needs that money."

"I see. Your concern is for the town."

"Well, of course my actions are not all selfless—yet, I *am* concerned for the people of this town," he admitted.

"I guess the people of Abilene are lucky to have you here, Mr. Coe."

"Your tone is sarcastic, Mr. Adams, but nevertheless your words are true. Enjoy yourself, and please excuse me."

I looked over at Hardin, who now seemed oblivious to everything else in the room except his cards. Sitting there with his back to the wall he reminded me of Hickok, who was doing exactly the same thing over at the Alamo.

I finished my beer, figuring there was nothing more to be learned here. The question as to whether or not they ran crooked games was no longer of any importance to me. Whatever had started Hickok and Coe at each other's throats was not important. What *was* important was that they were on a collision course that could tear the whole town apart.

13

The following day Jesse and Frank James pulled out of Abilene, having been true to their agreement with Hickok that they would lay low while in town. So now Ben Thompson was out of action, and the James boys were gone altogether. When things finally came to a head, they would not be around to add to it. If Wes Hardin were also to leave town, I would have felt much better.

That morning I told Bill what had happened last night after I'd left the Alamo.

"None of you recognized either one of those boys?" he asked afterward.

I shook my head. "I'd never even seen their faces in town, Bill."

He thought a moment. "You're of a mind that Phil Coe sent them, aren't you?" he asked finally.

"I am. Ben Thompson figured out why I was here, to back you up. He must have mentioned it to Coe. It might have been easier to get a couple of Texas cowhands to go after me than you. When the crunch comes, Coe would rather not have me backing you."

"Did he recognize your name when you first met him?" he asked.

"He said it sounded familiar, and I'm sure Ben filled him in later."

"It figures he'd be more afraid of you than either Williams or Carson," Bill commented.

"If he even knows about Carson," I added.

"He knows," Bill told me. "He knows most everything that goes on in this town."

"How's that?"

"I wish *I* knew," he replied.

We were in his office and I took a seat in the chair in front of his desk. "The James boys pulled up stakes," I said.

"I know. I saw them leave."

"That puts them and Thompson out of the picture. Now all we've got to worry about is Hardin."

"You gonna start that again?" he asked.

I told him what I saw in the Bull's Head last night, and what Coe told me about being friends with Hardin.

"I took some money off of Wes the other day," Bill told me. "I guess he decided the pickings would be easier at the Bull's Head. I can't blame him for that."

"What about him being friends with Coe?" I asked.

He wrinkled up his long nose. "I think that's more a case of his being friends with Ben Thompson, since they're both Texans."

I disagreed. "Bill, I think you've got a blind spot where that boy is concerned."

"That's not for you to say, Clint," he replied coldly.

In spite of his tone, I went on. "If I'm here to back you up, then it is for me to say."

"You afraid of facin' Wes?" he asked.

I frowned. "Bill, you know better than to ask me a

question like that. I may be cautious—but when have I been afraid to face anyone?"

He looked at me a moment, then a wry grin creased his handsome face and he slapped a palm down on his desk.

"Never!" he snapped. "I'm sorry, Clint, I don't know what came over me. Course you ain't afraid of nobody. Hell, you ain't even afraid of me."

For him, I thought, but never of him. He was changing, and I didn't like the changes.

"That's right, Bill. All I'm asking you to do is be more careful, that's all."

"Okay, so I'll be more careful," he agreed, spreading his arms out as if surrendering. He stood up then, saying, "I think I'll go over to the undertaker's and take a look at those two yahoos who shot at you last night. Maybe I'll recognize them."

"I'll walk with you."

On the way there he said, "You must have given Nell some workout last night, Clint. She didn't come back down 'til late, and she was glowin' like she had a lamp inside her head."

"We got along fine." That's all I'd tell him.

"I'm sure," he said, laughing.

At the undertaker's he took a look at the two men.

"Shotgun did a job on that jasper," he commented as we walked out. He seemed more thoughtful to me.

"Did you recognize them?" I asked.

For a moment I thought he might not have heard me, but then he said, "Uh—no, I didn't recognize them. Hell, there wasn't much of one of them to recognize anyways, was there?"

"No," I agreed, "your friend Mike let go with both barrels and blew him clear off the roof."

"I'm glad he was there to help you out, Clint."

"Carson came by, too, afterward. Said he was in the Bull's Head and heard the shotgun blast as he was coming out."

"What the hell was he doing in the Bull's Head?" he asked. "I told him to patrol the street."

I shrugged. "You'll have to ask him that, Bill."

"Damn right I will!" he snapped, angrily. "Let's get a drink."

I didn't want a drink, but I went with him anyway, thinking we were going to the Alamo. It didn't take me long to realize where Bill was heading for his drink.

We were going to the Bull's Head.

"Bill—" I started.

"We're just paying Coe a little visit, Clint. Don't get yourself in an uproar."

The Bull's Head was empty when we entered and what few customers were there looked up when they heard the doors swing open. The foam-favoring barkeep looked up also and frowned when he saw Hickok.

Bill walked right to the bar and ordered beer.

"Sure, Marshal," the bartender said. He looked at me and even though I didn't want one I told him, "The same."

"Where's Coe?" Bill asked.

"He hasn't come out yet, Marshal," the bartender replied, drawing the two beers.

I had a feeling I knew what Bill was planning, and I watched as the bartender drew the two beers. Sure enough, he brought them both over with a large head of foam on each.

"What do you call this?" Bill asked the bartender.

Frowning the man said, "Uh, that's beer, Marshal. You ordered beer."

"You call this beer?" Bill asked, pushing the glass so that some of the liquid sloshed out of the glass onto the bar. "Where's Coe?"

"I told you, Marshal—"

"Get him out here," Bill snapped. "I want to talk to him about this so-called beer."

"Marshal, he'll be out a little later."

Bill moved so quickly he surprised even me. He grabbed up the beer mug from the bar, whirled, and threw it across the room. It crashed into a wall and shattered, showering beer over some of the gambling devices in the room.

He whirled again, grabbed up my mug, and threw it the other way, where it struck a door and broke, spilling another shower of beer over that part of the room. I assumed that the door was the entrance to Coe's office, and I soon saw I was right.

The door swung open and an angry-looking Coe came storming out.

"What the hell—!" he was shouting, and stopped short when he saw Hickok. "Hickok, what the hell do you think you're doing?" he demanded.

Bill stayed where he was as Coe stormed across the room.

"I've warned you before, Coe. Your man is serving mugs of beer that are half foam. I also see men wearing guns in here. Your customers' guns are supposed to be collected when they come in."

"Marshal, I'm not gonna let you harass me in my own place," Coe warned, angrily. He was so angry his speech was slurred.

"I'm the law, Coe!" Bill shouted back. "I do what I want where I want. My friend here tells me someone tried to bushwhack him last night. You wouldn't know anything about that, would you?"

"You can't hang that on me, Hickok. If he's a friend of yours I'm sure some good Texans would think that was reason enough to backshoot him."

"There's no such thing as a good Texan," Hickok threw back at Coe.

"Get out of here, Hickok, before I forget that technically you are the law!" Coe snapped.

"I'm warning you, Coe. Any of my deputies, or my friends, catch a bullet, I'm coming after you," Hickok spat at Coe. Then he turned and said to me, "Let's go."

"You're gonna be finished in this town, Hickok. I promise you that," Coe yelled as we left. "You're finished!"

14

"Bill, that could make him come after you, you know," I told him outside.

"He'd never come after me himself," he said confidently. "He hasn't got the guts."

"I wouldn't push him too far on that assumption."

"He's been pushing me too long, Clint," he told me. "It's about time his hide got nailed to the wall."

"What if Hardin is in with him?"

"Then I'll nail him up, too."

We were walking down Texas Street and I asked, "You going back to your office?"

"Hell, no, I'm goin' to the Alamo to get a drink for real," he told me. "You want one?"

"No. Bill, I don't think you should—"

"Clint, do me a favor, will you?"

I shelved the remark I was about to make about his drinking and said, "What's that?"

"Find Tom Carson for me. Bring him to the Alamo. I want to find out just what the hell he thought he was doing last night in the Bull's Head."

"Where's he staying?"

"A boardinghouse on the south end of town. He'll either be there or at one of the whorehouses."

'I'll bring him."

"Thanks."

When we got to the Alamo Bill started to go in, then stopped short and turned around with a grin on his face.

"If I see Nell, I'll give her your love."

"Thanks a lot."

He went in and I kept walking, thinking about Carson. Was he working for Coe? Was that why he had volunteered for deputy duty, because Coe had sent him to keep an eye on Hickok?

When I reached the south end of town I saw the boardinghouse. There was no name on it, and no number, just a plain wooden door. I knocked and it was answered by an elderly woman with watery eyes.

"I'm looking for Tom Carson," I told her.

"Carson?" she asked. "He didn't come home last night that I know of. I'll bet he stayed in one of them sinful houses," she said disapprovingly.

"One of those sinful houses?" I repeated.

"Places where no God-fearing young girl would work, and no God-fearing young man would go," she announced. "You look like a sinner, young man. You must know where them places are."

"Yes, ma'am, as a matter of fact I do. Thank you."

"Sinner!" she cursed, and shut the door.

I turned around and walked back to the center of town, where the two largest cathouses were set up. I knocked on the door of the first, the one Hickok had told me was called Billie's—which must have been why it was his favorite.

The young girl who answered was wearing a robe that hung open revealing a fetching little figure with small, well-rounded breasts.

"Honey, we don't open until one," she told me,

eyeing me up and down, "but maybe Billie will let me make an exception in your case."

"Maybe another time," I told her. "Right now I'm looking for a man named Tom Carson. Is he here?"

"What do I know from names, honey?" she asked. She couldn't have been more than sixteen, and for some reason I started thinking of the girl Allie, over at the hotel. I hadn't had the opportunity to this point to get better acquainted with her. I'd have to see if I couldn't do something about that.

"You'd remember this guy, sweetheart. He'd be wearing a star on his chest," I told her, tapping my chest on the left side.

The look on her face changed and she said, "Oh, him. You a friend of his?" she asked.

"I hardly know him," I assured her.

"Well, he was here all right—for a while. When he started to get rough Billie had to ask him to leave. I think he went across the street. They got a couple of girls over there who go for that stuff."

"Okay, little girl, thanks."

She smiled again and said, "Sure, any time. C'mon back when you ain't busy. Ask for Alicia."

"Alicia. I'll remember. Have a good day."

"You gotta be kidding," she said and shut the door.

I guess that was a pretty silly thing to say to a whore, although I have known a few who have enjoyed their work.

I went across the street to a building with a big sign on the outside that said: LORD'S HOUSE OF ILL REPUTE. I didn't know if it was intended as blasphemy, or if the place was run by somebody named Lord.

The door was answered by a man, undoubtedly the bouncer, from the size of him. He was about six-four and surely weighed three hundred pounds. If Lord's House catered to the rough trade, it figured they'd have a bouncer like him.

"Yeah?" he asked.

"I'm looking for Deputy Tom Carson," I told him. "Is he here?"

"Who wants to know?" he asked.

I looked over my right shoulder, and then looked over my left. Then I looked back at him and said, "I guess I do."

His eyes locked with mine for a moment, then he backed away from the door. I took it as an invitation to enter. Once I was inside he closed the door behind us.

"Wait," he told me.

He went up a flight of steps and disappeared from view. A few minutes later Tom Carson appeared at the head of the stairs, tucking his shirt into his pants.

"What do you want, Adams?" he asked irritably. As he came down the steps I noticed that he had a couple of skinned knuckles on his right hand, and I took an instant dislike to the man. I never had any use for a man who would smack a woman around for enjoyment.

"The marshal wants you over at the Alamo," I told him.

"Yeah, tell him I'll be there in a little while."

"Now," I told him.

He frowned at me, then asked, "What's it about?"

"You'll find out when we get there. Get your hardware and let's go."

"It's about last night, ain't it?" he asked belligerently. "You told him I wasn't around while you was gettin' shot at?"

"I told him what happened, Carson, that's all."

"Shit. I ain't finished upstairs," he muttered.

"What do you want to do, skin the knuckles of your

left hand on the poor girl's cheek?" I asked him. "Carson, you get your gear and meet me out front in two minutes, or I'm going to come up there after you. If I do that, you're going to find out how these girls feel while you're pounding on them, having your fun."

I turned around and walked outside to wait for him. About a minute later he came walking out, buckling his gunbelt, mumbling something I couldn't understand.

We walked to the Alamo side by side, and after a while he stopped mumbling and stayed silent. When we reached the saloon he walked through the doors and I stayed outside. I leaned up against a post and waited for him to come back out. When he did, about five minutes later, he still had the star on his shirt. That's what I was waiting to see.

"Carson," I called as he walked out. When he turned to face me I could see that his face was red. "I see you're still wearing the badge."

"Look, Adams, I ain't—"

"Don't talk, Carson, just listen," I told him, and he shut up. "I've only got one thing to say to you. If I find out that you're working for Phil Coe or anyone else against Marshal Hickok, you're going to have to answer to me. That's a promise."

With that I turned and walked away, leaving him there to digest what I'd said right on top of whatever Bill had told him.

At the moment, though, I had something else in mind —I had decided to go on a picnic.

15

Allie Shaw was not as young as she appeared, although she was as sweet.

She had a room at the American House Hotel because her uncle was the manager. I got her room number from the other clerk, called on her, and asked her if she would do me the honor of accompanying me on a picnic. She said she would be delighted.

I went to the livery to rent a buggy, then to the general store to fetch picnic supplies, including a blanket and a wicker basket. For food I went to the dining room of the hotel and asked them for some fried chicken, some bread, a couple of bottles of wine, some cheese, napkins and cups.

I picked her up in the buggy and we drove out from the north end of town to a pond that the livery man told me about. It was a nice spot for a picnic.

Once we got there we began talking, and I steered the conversation around her. She was wearing a pink dress with a frilly neck and short sleeves. It was tied at the waist, emphasizing both her trim waist and her rounded breasts. When she sat on the ground she pulled her dress up, revealing lithe, smooth young legs. With a ribbon in her hair she looked even younger than I had first guessed, but after a few moments I discovered that she was actually twenty years old.

"You look much younger," I told her, but inwardly I was glad that she *was* at least twenty years old. As I approached forty, I became more conscious of young girls. I didn't mind young whores, but *nice* young girls made me nervous.

"I know I look younger," she told me. "I wish I could do something about it. Maybe I should cut my hair?" she wondered aloud. "Or wear it up? Or perhaps some rouge or powder?"

I cupped her chin and said, "Don't you dare do anything to that face," I told her. "You couldn't hope to make it more beautiful than it is right now."

She blushed and lowered her eyes. The difference between a girl like this and a woman like Nell Virdon was amazing. I was attracted to each one for different reasons. As soon as I saw Nell I knew I wanted her in bed, and I knew that we would end up there. With Allie it was different. Oh, I wanted to bed her, all right. But I wasn't sure we'd ever get there, and I had no intentions of pushing her into it. If it happened it would happen on its own.

She told me she had come to Abilene when she was eleven with her parents, after her uncle had become manager of the hotel. Both her parents had died a short time later, and she was brought up by her uncle. After a few years she began to work in the hotel for him.

"He treats me all right," she said. "Not like a father or anything like that, but he gives me a place to sleep and eat, and he doesn't abuse me in any way."

After that, she asked me about myself. She was very easy to talk to and I told her how I had come west as a young man and drifted into law work, how I became fascinated with guns and what made them work, how I became disenchanted with the job of keeping the peace when so many people were intent on breaking it, and how I had been traveling the past two years, living on money I had earned or won and whatever I picked up as a gunsmith.

"I've heard talk—" she began and then stopped.

"About what?" I asked.

She shook her head shyly, and said, "Never mind."

"No, if you have a question, Allie, ask it."

"It's just that I've heard talk that you are a good friend of Marshal Hickok's—and he's a notorious gunfighter."

"You mean, since I'm friends with Wild Bill Hickok, am I also a 'notorious gunfighter'?" I said, making the phrase sound like it was from a dime novel.

"You're making fun of me," she said, looking away.

"No, I'm not, really," I told her, touching her arm. "What do you think of me?" I asked her.

"I think you're very nice. You've acted like a perfect gentleman since you first arrived at the hotel."

"Then isn't that all that matters?"

"Yes, it is," she said firmly.

"Good. Since you feel that way, I'll answer your question. I am a friend of Bill Hickok's, and we've stood by each other many times when it came to using our guns. If that makes me a notorious gunman then I guess I'll just have to live with it."

That was the most relaxing afternoon I'd spent in a long while, and when I dropped her off in front of the hotel she expressed the hope that we could do it again some time.

"Perhaps we could have dinner together this evening?" I proposed.

"I'd like that, Clint, but I have to work the desk tonight," she said, looking disappointed.

"All right, Allie, we'll do it another time," I told her. "I'll see you later on this evening when I come in."

"Okay, Clint. Thank you for a wonderful afternoon."

"Thank you, Allie, it was a breath of fresh air that I needed very badly."

She blushed again and went inside.

I took the buggy back to the livery and was walking across Texas Street when I spotted Mike Williams coming down the street toward me.

"Where the hell have you been?" he demanded. But he wasn't belligerent—he was excited about something.

"What happened?" I asked him.

"All hell broke loose this afternoon. We've got one of Coe's men in jail."

"For what?"

"For shooting down a cattle man during an argument."

"Who arrested him? Bill?"

He shook his head. "You?"

He shook his head again and said—unnecessarily now: "Tom Carson."

My surprise must have shown on my face.

"That should prove that he's not working for Coe," Mike added as we hurried together to the jail.

"Yeah," I said sourly, thinking that maybe that was just the reason Carson had made the arrest.

16

"Where were you?" Bill asked as we entered his office.

"I was on a picnic," I told him. He didn't say anything to that, and I asked, "What's the story?"

"The feller in the cell got into an argument with one of the cattle boys over at the Alamo. It spilled out into the street, and this feller shot the other one dead. Carson came on the scene and arrested this feller, who works for Phil Coe."

"Does Coe know?" I asked.

"He was there," Carson spoke up. "He told this guy not to worry, that he'd get him out."

"How'd you happen to be there?" I asked Carson.

"That's my job," he shot back.

"This could push Coe over the edge," I told Wild Bill.

"I hope it does," he replied. "I hope that snake comes down here and tries to break his man out."

He looked at Williams and said, "Mike, I want you here at all times, now. Carson, you'll relieve him in twelve hours, and then he'll come back and relieve you. We'll work it that way until we can get rid of this jasper. Clint," he said, looking at me and opening his desk drawer, "I think it's time you put on a star. It's no secret why you'rc hcrc, and I need another deputy now."

Reluctantly I said, "All right, Bill." I took the badge from him.

When I pinned it to my chest it was the first time I had worn one in two years.

"You know the speech, Clint. Raise your right and swear to uphold the law."

"I do."

"Okay, you're deputized. I want you out on the streets where you'll do the most good."

I had the uncomfortable feeling that Bill was going to put himself where he thought he'd do the most good—right inside the Alamo.

"What about Coe?" I asked.

"What about him?" he said.

"You going to talk to him?"

"If I see him again, I might just kill him," Bill said with feeling.

"Then maybe I should talk to him," I offered.

"I'll lcave that up to you, Clint," he said. "You wanna waste your breath, you go right ahead."

"Talking to him just might avoid a confrontation," I tried to explain. But I had the impression Bill wasn't all that intent on avoiding a confrontation.

"Like I said, you wanna talk," Bill told me, "then talk."

He got up, which spelled an end to the meeting. Williams moved in and took his place at the desk, leaning his shotgun against it.

"I'll see you in twelve," Carson told him, and he went out.

"Has it occurred to you that this might be a set-up to make Carson look good?" I asked Bill.

"It could be," Bill agreed.

"Who was the man killed?"

"One of the cowhands who came in with a drive in the past few days."

"Was he a Texan?" I asked.

"How am I supposed to know that?" he asked.

"The way Coe feels about Texans, I don't think this man will turn out to be from Texas, otherwise Coe wouldn't have sacrificed him. Besides, arresting a man who killed a Texan would make you look too good," I told him.

"So, find out if he *was* a Texan," Bill barked. "I'm going over to the Alamo. Come over later on. Nell was asking for you this morning."

"I'll come by," I promised. I decided to do just what Bill suggested. I was going to find out if the dead man was a Texan, or if he was just a cowhand who had hired on for the drive.

17

I asked around town, and many people had already heard about the shooting in front of the Bull's Head. In spite of what I had told Bill, I did not go and talk to Coe—yet. Instead, I hit some of the smaller saloons in town, and I finally learned what outfit the dead man—whose name turned out to be Rafe Morgan—had been working for.

The outfit was called the Flying Z, and they were camped south of town. I went to the livery and saddled Duke, who seemed to appreciate the opportunity for some exercise. The big horse had never liked being cooped up for any length of time, and he was rightfully upset with me for neglecting him.

As we rode into camp Duke commanded a lot of attention because cattlemen not only know cows, they know good horseflesh, too. And Duke had plenty of that.

There was a certain degree of tension in the camp, however, which was not a surprise, considering one of their number had been gunned down in the streets of Abilene that same day.

As I rode into their camp I was eventually challenged by the man I took to be their foreman. He was

massive, just short of being as big as the bouncer in
Lord's House. He had wide shoulders, bulging arms
and powerful legs. He was some thick around the
middle, but it was muscle, not fat. He appeared to be
in his mid-thirties, although his dark hair was pep-
pered with gray. He wore a Navy Colt on his hip,
both gun and holster appearing well-worn. He was
not a gunslick, however, for he wore the gun too high
on his hip.‘ To him it was just another article that he
had to put on in the morning when he got dressed.

"Howdy," he greeted me, but there was a wealth of
suspicion hidden in that one word.

"Afternoon," I said. "Mind if I step down for a
spell?"

I had the feeling that at that particular moment he
first took notice of the badge on my chest. He
squinted at it, then stood up straight and said, "That
depends on what you have in mind."

"A couple of questions, is all." Gradually I was
being enclosed in a circle of men, but I didn't feel as
if I were in any immediate danger. More than anything else they were just curious.

" 'Bout what?"

"About Rafe Morgan."

"Rafe's dead, got shot down in the street," he said.
"You should know that."

"I do know it. We've got the killer in jail," I said.

They exchanged glances now, and then he said,
"That ain't the way we hear it. Seems to me Bill
Hickok just took the chance to lock up a Texan in
that jail of his."

I ignored that remark. "Were any of you present
when Morgan was shot?" I asked.

There was a grumbling working its way through
the crowd, but no one stepped forward with an an-

swer. I decided to try another question.

"Can you tell me if Morgan was a Texan?"

Again, no answer.

"Look, I'm asking you—"

"You look," the big foreman said. "We know who you are, and we know you've got a hot rep with a gun." He held his big ham-like fists out to me and asked, "How are you with your hands?"

"What's that got to do with anything?" I asked.

"We don't like gunslingers," he told me. "You've got a marshal who's a gunslinger, and you've got a deputy who's a gunslinger," he said, meaning me. "A gun don't make you a man. Maybe you got to prove to us that you're a man before we'll answer any of your questions."

Looking at him I doubted that I could fight him and come out a winner, but I wanted the information on Morgan.

"All right, but look—" I started to say, dismounting. I didn't get any further. He reached up with his big hands to help me dismount and before I knew it I was flying through the air and coming down on the hard ground with a bang that knocked the wind out of me. They all started laughing, and through a kind of a haze I noticed somebody moving Duke so he wouldn't be in the way.

I had landed on my back, and now I rolled over and got to my knees. The big foreman was advancing on me, a smile on his face and a gleam in his eye. Apparently he was a brawler, and he loved every minute of it.

He launched a kick at me and I immediately rolled to the left to avoid being decapitated. The force of his intended kick was so great that when he missed, his other foot went out from under him and he came down hard on his keester. That gave me a few seconds to try and get my wind back, which I did in big, gulping breaths.

I got to my feet before he did, but I waited for him to get up and make his move. I wanted him coming at me, not lying in wait for me.

He got up laughing and turned to face me. The crowd of men were shouting encouragement to him now, and we circled each other slowly. Finally he charged me. But he seemed to have anticipated my move, because as I jumped to the right, he swung a vicious backhand that caught me in the right cheek as he went by. I felt the skin on my skin split and the blood trickle down my cheek as I lost balance, falling to one knee.

He was faster than he looked. He reversed direction quickly and came after me before I could regain my balance. He hit me with his shoulder and knocked me sprawling into the dirt.

When he came at me again I lifted my right foot and planted it in his gut and, bracing myself against the ground with both hands, I pushed. I staggered back a few steps, but not as far as I would have liked. He probably could have caught me again before I got to my feet, but he allowed me to get up and we stood facing each other once again.

I decided to go on the offensive this time and it caught him by surprise. I threw several lefts and rights that landed solidly. One caught him square in the right eye, which began to puff up immediately.

That didn't seem to faze him, though, because he was still laughing as he swung a right that caught me in the left rib section. I could have easily gone down from the pain, but I gritted my teeth and stayed on my feet, throwing another right hand. I caught him in the mouth as he was laughing and his bottom lip split, spraying blood on my shirt front that mingled there with the blood from my split cheek.

I backed away from him then and we circled each other warily. Breathing was a painful thing for me, but I was gratified to see that his eye was closing, his lip was bleeding, and he also seemed to be breathing hard.

Damned if he wasn't still smiling, though!

He stepped toward me and swung a big right which I ducked under. I threw a couple of rights and lefts to his midsection, which seemed to be as hard as a rock, but was satisfied again when I heard him grunt.

Suddenly I knew I'd made a mistake by ducking beneath his sweeping right. He brought both arms around and caught me in a powerful bear hug. His biceps felt like boulders as they pressed against my ribs. He lifted me up off my feet and I dangled there, helpless, as he proceeded to squeeze the breath—and very possibly the life—out of me.

It was still daylight, but I was seeing stars. My arms were free from the bear hug, but I couldn't use them to pry his arms apart. As I continued to struggle we bumped heads accidentally and I heard him grunt. Hearing that, I closed my eyes and pulled my head back as far as I could, then brought it forward as hard as I could, knowing full well that I might succeed in knocking myself out.

Apparently, however, his head was not as hard as the rest of him, because when my forehead struck his forehead, his skin split open and he bellowed in pain. The blood began to trickle down his face and into his eyes and mouth. As he spit it from his mouth it struck me in the face. The move did not break his bear hug, but weakened it considerably. The only other thing I could think to do was cup my hands and slap them together over his ears, which had to sting.

As I did so he yelled again and his arms loosened enough for me to slide through. I did and got back on my feet. Once there I brought my knee up, hoping to cripple him with a shot to the groin. He sensed my intention, though, and he swiveled his hips around so that my knee struck his thigh, having no effect. Before he could catch me in another hug I danced away from him, getting some breathing and maneuvering room.

I watched him as he shook his head, trying to clear his face of the blood that was pouring down from his forehead. It was not a serious injury, but it was bleeding like hell and I knew I had to get him while he couldn't see me. I took a good running start and drove my shoulder into his midsection, knocking him down and going down with him.

When we hit the ground, kicking up a massive cloud of dirt and dust, I rolled away from him quickly as he tried to gather me up in his arms again. I tried to figure out where to hit him next to do the most damage, and as he struggled to his knees he presented me with his broad back. I launched myself shoulder-first into the small of his back, knocking him sprawling once again, this time on his face.

The impact caused some pain to shoot through my shoulder, and I knew that if I did something like that again, I'd have to use the other shoulder.

I was so tired I couldn't even get off my knees. As he struggled again to get to his feet I threw a left hand at him that caught him on the cheek and rocked his head back. He retaliated by throwing a right hand that caught me on the forehead, knocking me flat on my back. The next thing I knew he had leaped on me, the full weight of his body driving what little breath I had left out of my lungs in a great rush.

The last thing I saw was him sitting up on my chest, face streaming with blood that dripped off his chin. He drew back his right hand and threw a punch that I never saw land. . . .

As I came out of it I was dimly aware of someone handing me a canteen, and from instinct I opened it and poured it over my head. The water was cold and helped to clear my head, which was pounding. I felt my face, trying to find the place where his last punch landed, but I couldn't distinguish one lump from the next.

"What happened?" I asked. "Where'd that last punch land?"

"It didn't," I heard someone say. I turned my head and saw the foreman sitting next to me. Apparently he had just emptied a canteen over his own head, because blood mingled with water was pouring off his chin. "I was about to throw it when you passed out. I guess you couldn't breathe with me sitting on your chest."

His face was a mess. His right eye was closed, he had a gash on his forehead that was still leaking blood, and his bottom lip was badly split.

"You don't look so good either," he told me. I felt my face again, locating the split cheek and various other lumps, but both of my eyes seemed to be open and I seemed to have all my teeth, although a few felt loose. I took a swig from the canteen and ran some water around my mouth. When I spit it out it was a thin, red stream.

"I don't feel so good, either," I told him.

"Neither do I, friend," he told me.

Friend? Hadn't I lost the fight?

"My name's Moose," he told me, which didn't surprise me. He held his hand out and we shook gingerly, since both of our hands were kind of tender. I was glad to see my right hand wasn't all that swollen. I could still fire my gun if I had to.

"I don't understand," I told him. "I thought I had to win the fight—"

A few of the men began laughing and so did Moose.

"Hell, mister, nobody expected you to win," he told me. "But then nobody expected you to bust me up the way you done. No, sir, you proved you're a man, even without your gun."

He took a swig of water and spit out a red stream as I had. "Now what were them questions you wanted answered?"

18

It was getting dark as I rode back to town. My whole body ached, but I had found out what I wanted.

Morgan was not a Texan. He had signed on with the drive in Oklahoma and had not made any friends during the ride. As to the second question, there wasn't a Flying Z man in town at the time Morgan was getting himself shot.

The whole incident could very well have been rigged to make Bill look bad by arresting a Texan—even though the actual arrest had been made by Tom Carson.

When we reached town I took Duke to the livery and practically fell off of him. My ribs were sore on the left side, and I wasn't all that sure that there wasn't something busted up inside. First order of business would be to find the doctor.

"What the hell happened to you?" the livery man asked.

"I just had a conversation with somebody who wasn't much of a talker," I told him. "Where do I find the doctor?"

"You don't," he told me.

"What do you mean, I don't?" I asked. "If I don't,

I'm liable to fall apart in little tiny pieces."

He shrugged apologetically. "Doc just took his buggy out and went to the Miller place. Miz Miller's havin' a baby."

"A baby," I repeated. I was standing on my own two feet, but I felt strangely as if I were floating above the ground. I marveled at how Moose had been able to shake off the effects of our battle and still have the strength to lift me up and plant me in my saddle.

"With him out of town, what's the closest we've got to a doctor?" I asked.

He thought a moment. "Allie Shaw, at the American House," he told me. "She helps Doc sometimes, when he needs some kind of a nurse."

"She didn't go with him to help with the baby?" I asked.

"She usually does, but not this time."

"Okay, thanks."

I took a tentative step and almost fell. He grabbed me and asked, "You gonna make it, Mr. Adams?"

"I'll make it," I told him. I took a deep breath to clear my head, then took another step. That one worked, so I took one more. Everytime one worked, I took another, until I was at the hotel and walking into the lobby.

Allie was working the desk and she looked up with a ready smile on her face, expecting a customer. When she saw me her face fell, and she cried out, "Clint, what happened?"

She rushed around the desk and ran to me, grabbing hold of my left arm to hold me up. "You're all covered with blood," she told me, unnecessarily.

"It's not all mine," I told her, as if that would be some comfort.

"Oh, Doc's not in town," she lamented.

"I know it, that's why I came to you."

"I'll take care of you," she promised. "Let's get you upstairs."

We staggered up the stairs together and she opened a door and helped me into a room.

"This isn't my room," I told her.

"No, it's mine," she told me. "It's closer."

I was going to argue, but she guided me to her bed and when I fell on it I knew I didn't have the strength to get up again.

"Let me get some warm water and cloths," she said. "Just rest, I'll be right back."

I must have fallen asleep, because when I woke up my shirt was off and so were my boots. Allie was sitting next to the bed, washing the blood from my face and neck.

"You'll have a scar on your cheek," she said.

"It won't be my first," I assured her.

"How did this happen?" she asked.

"Just a little fight."

"A little fight?" she asked, incredulously. "With how many men?"

"Just one," I told her. "A Moose."

"A moose?"

I smiled at her, even though it made my face hurt.

"It's a man's name," I said. "And it fit him."

We both looked down at my left side, where there was a livid bruise larger than a hand.

"What hit you there?" she asked, feeling around. I flinched at the pain and she apologized.

"A man's fist," I told her.

"I thought it must be a club or something," she commented, still probing. "That hurt?" she asked.

"Some."

"If you had cracked ribs it would hurt like the devil," she told me.

She probed again and I assessed the amount of

pain. I decided that it did not hurt like the devil, so
we agreed that I probably didn't have cracked ribs.

"This cut on your face looks like the worst of it,"
she told me. "It crosses the other scar." She eyed me
critically and said, "Cleaned up you don't look too
bad. When you first walked in you looked half-
dead."

"I felt it, too," I told her. "Allie?"

"Yes?"

"Thanks."

I started to get up and she put her hand against my
chest and said, "Whoa, mister, where do you think
you're going?"

"I'm going back to my own room."

"You're gonna spend the night right where you
are," she said firmly.

"My room is only down the hall, Allie," I insisted,
trying to get up again.

Shaking her head she pushed me back down. "I'm
the doc while Doc's away. And you're my patient. I
say you're staying."

"But I'm fine," I said. "I can walk."

She stood up with both hands on my chest, pushing
down on me. Her face was very close to mine as she
said, "Did it ever occur to you that I might have some
other reason?"

I thought about that, and while I did she removed
her hands and gathered up the basin and the cloths
she'd used to clean me.

"You get some rest," she said finally. "I'll look in
on you later, to make sure you're all right."

She blew out the lamp and left me in the dark,
wondering if she meant what I thought she meant.

19

I didn't know what time it was when she came back. It was pitch black, and I couldn't even see her.

I came awake, aware that she was in the room. First I smelled her, the clean, fresh scent of her hair and her skin. Then I heard her, the soft whisper of her bare feet on the floor. After that, I felt her.

Her hands snaked beneath the sheet and touched my chest. I was about to speak when I realized something. This was out of character for her. She was being very bold, and she was probably a virgin. That meant she was nervous. I decided the best thing for me to do was keep quiet and let her feel her way around.

She ran her hands over my chest lightly at first, then they roamed down over my belly, light as a feather. I began to react further down, as she'd soon find out. She went from my belly down lower, all right, but she circled around the vital spot and began to feel my thighs. First the tops of my thighs, then the insides. Finally, she decided to throw caution to the wind. She touched my penis, then pulled her hands away. Then they came back, tentatively, stroking and touching. Finally there was a sharp intake of breath as she grasped it tightly in her fist.

When her hand left me I knew she'd decided that it was time to go all the way.

She pulled the sheet back and climbed into bed next to me. Her legs touched mine, and the flesh was burning hot. Her breasts brushed my chest, the nipples already swollen with desire.

I felt her breath on my face, and I sought her mouth with mine. She responded tentatively at first, then avidly, her mouth opening, accepting my tongue, then using her own. Her hands roamed over my body again, clutching at my buttocks, pinning my erection between us.

For a while the only active part I took was to kiss her while her hands probed and inspected and investigated. When I'd had enough of that I ran my hands over her round little breasts and played with the nipples while she caught her breath and moaned. I began to kiss her neck, her shoulders, and then ran my lips over her breasts and my tongue over her nipples. That seemed to drive her crazy. Her nipples appeared to be very sensitive. When I bit them she groaned and grasped my head, holding it tightly against her.

After a while I moved my hands down over her belly to the mound of hair between her legs. I scratched and pulled on the hair, then probed lower, until my fingers split her and entered her. I inserted one finger first, then two, and she got wetter and wetter. She began grinding her crotch against my hand, and then, while I still had two fingers inside her, I found her clit with my thumb and began to rub it gently.

Her behind bounced off the bed and she kept repeating, "Oh . . . oh . . . oh . . ." over and over again.

I removed the two fingers I'd had inside of her, slick from her juices, and used them and my thumb to manipulate her button. She began to groan and sob invitingly, and I knew it was time.

I moved one leg over her, then straddled her. I found her entrance with my tip and inserted it gently. I slid in easily because she was so wet, but soon encountered the resistance of her maidenhead. I covered her mouth with mine securely, then thrust again, breaking through the barrier and entering deeply into her.

She cried out into my mouth, first in pain, and then in pleasure as I kept thrusting in and out, in and out. I moved my hands underneath her, cupping the globes of her buttocks, pulling her even more tightly to me. Her hands came around to my ass, imitating my action. She began to strain off the bed, trying to meet my thrusts with equal thrusts, and she was throwing the rhythm off. By using my hands on her rear I showed her the proper tempo, and then when she got the hang of it, it got better for both of us.

She began to cry again when she climaxed, and then when I came she clenched her teeth to keep from screaming—but I could feel the cords in her neck standing out.

When I went to withdraw from her, she held me fast, using her hands, and her legs, as she wrapped them around my back.

"No," she said, which was the only real word she had used the whole time.

I stayed inside of her, growing soft now, and we both fell asleep that way.

20

In the morning I left her, and the position she was in on the bed reminded me of Nell Virdon. There was such a difference between the two of them, yet I enjoyed them both. Nell would understand that, but I didn't know if Allie would. Not at this point in her life, anyway.

I was going to have a talk with her real soon, so that she didn't misunderstand what last night had meant.

Bill wasn't in his office, but Tom Carson was. He seemed to take great delight in my condition.

"Well, well, that's one fight I'm sorry I missed," he told me.

"Wish I could say the same. Any problems here?"

He shrugged. "The prisoner doesn't like the food, that's about it."

"Uh-huh." I was about to tell him what I had found out last night, but decided against him. If he was working for Coe, there was no point in making him think I was on to him.

"I'll see you later," I told him. He waved, as if he wasn't too thrilled with the idea. Neither was I.

I went over to the Alamo and found Bill in his customary spot, the same tables with his back against the same wall. There were no other players at the table, though, so he was just shuffling cards.

I sat down and took twenty dollars worth of chips, and he started dealing a hand.

"What the hell happened to you?" he asked. He dealt me an ace up, and himself a king up. I bet ten and he called.

"I got the answers to some questions, but I had to do it the hard way."

"It looks like it," he observed, dealing me a ten of hearts, to match the ace, and himself another king.

"Two dollars," he said.

"I call. Rafe Morgan is not a Texan," I told him, and I explained how he had hooked up with the herd in Oklahoma and made no friends.

"So you think that means that Coe set it up?" he asked.

I watched him deal me a three of hearts, and himself another king. He bet two dollars again, and I called.

"None of the Flying Z hands were in town that night. They're all Texans, and as far as they know you've locked up a Texan. That's all they care about."

He dealt himself an ace, and me a four of hearts. He bet two dollars, I raised him two, and he called.

"What are you going to do, Bill?" I asked.

He dealt us each our seventh cards, and then said, "I'm gonna bet into you, Clint."

He threw a five-dollar chip in. I had eleven dollars left, so I called and raised six.

"I'll call," he said.

I turned over my first two hole cards, which were aces. I didn't even turn over the other card, which was the fifth heart, because I knew I didn't need the flush to beat him. Just the three aces. He squinted across the table as if he couldn't believe his eyes.

He shook his head in wonder and threw in his hand. I raked in the chips and repeated, "What are you going to do?"

"I'm gonna wait, old friend," he told me. "If Coe's behind it, then sooner or later he'll try to spring his man."

"When do you figure?"

"There's a big cattleman's fair on October fifth," he told me. "Probably between now and then, if not on that day."

"Jesus Christ," I said, "this town will be swarming with Texans on the fifth."

"That's why I figure he might wait until then."

"That's only three days away, Bill."

He shrugged.

"This is more than just you and Coe," I said. "This could tear the whole town apart."

"That'll be up to Coe," he told me.

I gathered up the cards, not revealing that third hole card. Bill wouldn't like it if he knew I had him figured right from the start. He prided himself on his card-playing almost as much as he did on his ability to handle a gun.

I stood up and he said, "You gonna walk off with my money?"

I cashed in the chips and told him, "Take it out of my salary."

"Where you going, Clint?"

"Since you're intent on butting heads with Coe, maybe I can talk him out of it. Or maybe Ben Thompson can."

He shook his head, as if he doubted it, and pitied

me for wanting to give it a try.

I started to walk out when a woman called my name. I turned and saw Nell on the stairway.

"Well, what happened to you?" she asked.

I touched my face and then said, "All in the line of duty, ma'am."

She walked up to me and said, "Oh, I don't mean that. I mean what *happened* to you. Where have you been?"

"Oh. Well, I've been kind of busy. I'm sorry I haven't been around."

"Well try and fix that tonight, will you?" she asked me, touching my face. "I thought we had something special you know?"

"Sure, I'll try and get by tonight," I said, puzzled.

"I'll give you some tender loving care," she promised.

I smiled at her and left.

Was Nell going to be a problem, as well as Allie? I thought for sure she'd understand that "what we had" didn't mean anything past that one night.

What I didn't need was trouble from two women while I was trying to keep the lid on Abilene.

21

"There's nothing I can do, Clint," Ben Thompson told me from his bed in the American House Hotel.

"You mean there's nothing you want to do," I said. "Ben, this whole town's future could be affected by what happens between Coe and Hickok. You've got to talk to Coe."

"Have you talked to Hickok?" he asked. His face looked drawn and pale, and I was sure he was in pain —physical and emotional. His wife's arm had had to be amputated. The one thing he had to be grateful for was that his son's injury had not been very serious.

"I talked to Bill, but he's stubborn."

"So's Phil. It wouldn't do any good, Clint, I'm telling you."

"Well, what about Hardin?" I asked.

"What about him?"

"Was he imported to kill Hickok?"

He frowned, then made the decision to come clean. "We asked him to kill Hickok when he got here, Clint. He said no. He said why didn't I just do it myself."

"Why didn't you?"

"I'd just rather someone else did it, that's all," he told me.

His gun was hanging on the bedpost, within easy reach, and I was reminded again about how fast he really was.

"I'm out of it, Clint. That's the best I can do for you."

And I was grateful for that much.

"I'll talk to Coe myself," I told him, heading for the door.

"It won't do you any good," he said.

"You sound like Hickok." Before leaving I said, "I'm sorry about your wife, Ben."

He nodded, and I left.

Allie was behind the counter and I went over to talk to her.

"How do you feel?" she asked.

"Fine. I had a good nurse."

"And I had a good teacher," she said, blushing.

"Allie, we have to talk," I said.

"No we don't," she assured me. "I don't expect anything of you beyond last night, Clint, if that's what you're worried about."

I was surprised. "Well, it isn't that I was worried," I told her. "I just didn't want to hurt you."

"You wouldn't hurt me," she said. "I know that."

"Thanks, Allie—for understanding."

She smiled and said, "Maybe I'll see you later, hm?"

"Possibly. I'm going to be very busy."

"I told you, I don't expect anything from you. Just what you want to give me."

I patted her hand, smiled, and left.

That had been the attitude I would have expected to get from Nell Virdon, but things seemed to be reversed. Nell was the one who wanted more from me. Well, at least I wouldn't have to worry about Allie.

I went to the Bull's Head next and found Coe seated at one of the poker tables. He was alone.

"Coe—" I began, approaching him.

"Get out of here, Adams, and take that tin star with you," he spat.

I grabbed him by the lapels and hoisted him to his feet. "What the hell?" he began. I gave him a running start towards the door of his office and said, "Let's go inside, where we can talk."

The bartender had started around the bar and I pointed a finger at him and said, "I'd stay behind there if I was you, friend. You make a smaller target that way."

He took my words to heart and remained where he was. I turned back to Coe and said, "Inside."

He hesitated, then opened the door viciously and stalked into his office. I followed and closed the door behind us.

He seated himself behind his desk and I said, "If you've got a gun in one of those desk drawers don't bother going for it. I came here to talk, not to fight."

"So, talk."

"This thing between you and Hickok has to stop, Coe. It's going to end with the destruction of the whole town."

"That's up to Hickok."

It was amazing how much alike two men who hated each other could sound.

"He's the one who's going to have to back off, not me," he added.

"Dammit, neither one of you is going to back off!" I snapped.

"I don't mind that at all, Adams. My aim is to rid this town of Wild Bill Hickok."

"And destroy it in the process."

He scoffed at that possibility. "Is that all you came to talk about?"

"That's it," I said helplessly. "Except for Tom Carson."

"Carson," he said, frowning. "He's one of Hickok's deputies. What do you want to talk to me about him for?"

"Because I think he works for you, Coe. If I find out that you used a badge to work against Hickok, there won't be enough of you left for Bill to spit on."

I left him with his mouth hanging open and walked out.

"You better practice staying behind that bar, friend," I reminded the bartender on the way out.

Out on Texas Street I stood, shaking my head. Coe and Hickok seemed so intent on destroying each other they didn't care how much damage they did to get it done. I went over to Hickok's office to see the prisoner.

"Take a break, Tom," I told Carson as I walked in.

"What?"

"I said take a break. Come back in an hour or so, I'll cover for you."

He didn't have to be told again. He got up, grabbed his gunbelt and took off.

I went in the back with a stool, set it down and sat in front of the cell with Rafe Morgan's accused killer inside.

"What's your name?" I asked.

He was lying on his bunk and rolled over. "Who're you?" he asked.

"My name's Adams, Clint Adams. I'm sure you've heard it once or twice over the past few days."

"Yeah, I've heard."

"What's your name?"

"Landon, Whit Landon," he told me.

From what I could see he was about thirty or so, not overly tall, and slim.

"How long you working for Coe, Landon?" I asked.

He shrugged, seeing nothing wrong with answering the question. "Couple of weeks is all."

"Doing what?"

"This and that."

"You ever kill a man before?"

"Before when?" he asked.

"Before yesterday?"

"I didn't kill nobody yesterday."

"Aren't there witnesses?"

"To what?" he asked.

"The shooting," I said.

"What shooting?"

"The one you're arrested for," I answered.

"How would I know, I wasn't even there."

He was well schooled, and I wasn't about to get anything out of him.

"I understand," I told him. I picked up the stool and walked back into the office.

There were no witnesses to the killing at all. Hickok only had Carson's word that Whit Landon had done the shooting, because Carson made the arrest, and Bill was going along with it. Coe was probably planning to incite some good old Texas boys to help him break another Texan out of jail, and that's what Bill was preparing for.

I sat at Bill's desk, waiting for Carson to come back. When he did he was carrying a bottle and a smile.

"Beat up another whore, Carson?" I asked.

"You ain't gonna rile me, Adams, so why don't

you just get up outta that chair and let me get back to work."

"Tom, how many witnesses were there to that shooting?" I asked him.

"Witnesses? How the hell should I know? Ask the marshal."

"But you made the arrest."

"Well, I heard the shots, and when I got there this jasper was standing over the dead guy, and his gun was still smoking."

"This gun?" I asked. I opened the bottom drawer of Bill's desk and took out the prisoner's .45.

"Yeah, that's the gun."

I put the gun to my nose and smelled it, checked the cylinder, and found it fully loaded.

"This gun's fully loaded, Tom."

"So he reloaded it."

"This gun hasn't been fired in some time. Believe me, I can tell."

He looked annoyed. "Adams, that ain't none of my affair. That's up to the marshal. Now why don't you let me get back to work."

I put the gun back and stood up.

"Okay, Tom, you go back to work. You work real hard at guarding that prisoner. We wouldn't want anything to happen to an innocent man. At least, not until I can find the guilty one to put in there instead of him."

"Shit," he cursed, sitting down with his bottle.

Maybe he was wondering if he'd gotten in too deep. I hoped he was.

22

There were a lot of games being played in Abilene, and I seemed to be the only one who didn't want to go along.

I wondered if Wes Hardin wanted to play, or if he was just going to end up as a disinterested bystander. He was still in town, but he was keeping a low profile. From what I knew about Hardin, that wasn't in keeping with his character. The fact that I'd taken an instant dislike to him had kept me from having any kind of a conversation with him up until this point, but maybe it was time we did have a talk.

I knew if he wasn't staying at the American House, he had to be staying at one of the smaller hotels in town. I could have found out by asking Bill, but I didn't want to clash with him over Hardin. He had taken a liking to the young killer, one which I could probably understand if I tried hard enough.

I checked two or three of the smaller hotels in town before trying the American House.

"Yes, sir, Mr. Hardin is registered," the clerk told me.

"What room?"

"Second floor front, 201," he answered.

"Is he in?"

"I haven't seen him go out, sir."

"Okay, thanks."

I went up the stairs, located room 201 and knocked on the door.

"Yeah?" his voice called out.

"It's Adams."

There was a long pause, then he called out, "Come on in."

I opened the door and walked in and I was looking down the barrel of John Wesley Hardin's Colt .45.

"You're cautious, aren't you, boy?" I asked.

He stared at me, then eased the cocked hammer down on his gun and put it back in the holster on the bedpost.

"Ain't that how you stayed alive to a ripe old age?" he asked, emphasizing the word "old," which must have been in payment for my having called him "boy."

"Yep, that's how I did it, all right. Mind if I sit down?" I asked.

"Pull up a chair."

He was sitting up in bed, and now he leaned back against the headboard.

"Sleeping late?"

"Bastard in the next room snores so loud it keeps me awake all night," he complained. "Sooner or later I'm gonna put a bullet through this wall."

"I hope not."

"What's on your mind?" he asked. Then he added, "Deputy?" when he spotted the star.

"You are on my mind, Hardin. I can't help but wonder just what you're after here in Abilene. And now that I've been deputized, I figure I got the right to ask."

"Well," he said thoughtfully, putting his hands behind his head, "you figure wrong."

"How's that?"

"Hickok's the marshal," he told me, "and if and when he asks me, I'll give him a straight answer."

"How about giving me one straight answer, and then I'll go?" I asked.

"What's the question?"

"Did you come to Abilene to kill Wild Bill Hickok?"

"No," he said without hesitation.

I got up from my chair and walked out without a further word. The way he answered me made me believe him.

Later on, I was to remember the remark he made about the snoring man in the next room.

23

Abruptly I decided that I'd been running around much too much. I decided to head over to the Alamo for a few beers and a few hands of poker and a few hours—or more—of Nell Virdon.

The Alamo was in full swing and I went right to the bar to order a beer. Nell was there and she sidled over to me and said, "Glad you made it."

"I need some relaxation," I told her.

"Well, it's a little early to go upstairs, but there's an open seat at Bill's table," she told me.

I declined. "I'll wait for an opening at the other table. I don't like the idea of bumping heads with Bill, whether with cards or with guns."

I did take my beer over to Bill's table to watch, though, and I found out what had been bothering me for a while. Bill seemed to have trouble seeing the cards on the other end of the table. I'd noticed him squinting before, but it hadn't registered for what it was.

Bill was having trouble with his eyes.

I watched him more closely now, with that in mind, and it became increasingly clear. At times he even had trouble reading his own cards.

His erratic behavior—at least in part—could have been put down as a result of his eye problem. With that preying on his mind, he may not have been thinking right.

I knew he damn well wasn't seeing right, and I was going to have to talk to him about it pretty soon. I didn't want him thinking he had to go out in one last blaze of glory just because he was having some eye problems.

Of course, the major problem would be getting him to admit it.

"Pull up a chair, Clint," he invited. I didn't want to play him, but I didn't want to refuse and sit at the other table.

I drew fifty dollars worth of chips and played half-heartedly. Every time it looked as if it might come down to Bill and me, I dropped out. Still, when Nell gave me the sign that it was time to go up, I still had half my money in front of me.

"Cash me in," I told the dealer.

"Hey, the night's young," Bill told me.

"And I have other plans," I told him, looking towards Nell. He turned his head in the direction of my gaze, and then nodded and said, "Okay, boy. I'll hold down the fort here."

"Thank you."

I picked up my money and followed Nell upstairs.

In her room she turned into my arms, saying, "I've been waiting for this ever since the first time."

She covered my mouth with hers and began to unbutton my shirt frantically.

I found the zipper on her gown and pulled it down, then placed my hands against the bare flesh on her back.

That's when we heard the first shot.

"What was that?" she asked.

"It was a shot."

The second report followed soon after.

"I've got to check on it," I told her, buttoning my shirt. "I'm sorry, Nell."

"That's all right," she assured me, "just hurry back."

I opened her door and rushed down the stairs, through the crowded saloon.

"Clint!" I heard Bill call from behind me, but I kept on going right out the doors. I only hoped he didn't have such a good hand that he wouldn't follow me. I knew that he couldn't have heard the shots over the noises in the saloon.

Out on the street I stopped to listen for more shots, but none came. One more would have helped me locate the source, but I'd have to do without.

Actually, locating the source didn't turn out to be very hard, because there were loud voices coming from the American House Hotel, and right away I started thinking about Allie.

I started running in that direction just as the other clerk, Homer, came running out.

"Oh, thank God!" he shouted when he saw me. "I was just looking for the marshal."

"What's going on, Homer?" I asked.

"I don't know. We heard the shots and we don't know what's happening!"

"Where'd they come from?" I asked.

"I don't know, I don't know," he babbled nervously.

"Homer, calm down and think!" I snapped. "Where did the shots come from?"

"Okay, uh, second floor, I think. Yes, that's it, the second floor in the front."

I looked up. "Hardin's room," I said.

"What?"

"Nothing. Look, stay out here. If Hickok comes along send him upstairs."

"Yes, very well."

I went into the hotel and saw Allie behind the desk.

"Are you all right?" I asked her.

"I'm fine, Clint."

"Okay, just stay there," I told her, starting for the stairs.

"Be careful!" she called after me.

As I reached the top of the stairs I took my gun out and stood stock still, listening. When I didn't hear anything I began to work my way down the hall towards Hardin's room. When I reached his door I put my ear to it but could hear no sounds inside. When I turned the knob I found the door locked. I backed off and then hit the door with my foot, popping it open.

There was no one inside.

I felt a breeze and noticed the window was open. Hardin must have taken off through the window, but why? I sniffed at the air in the room, and there were still traces enough to tell me that a gun had been fired.

I looked around to see where the shots had gone. There was no blood, so there was no evidence that Hardin might be walking around with a bullet in him. If he wasn't shot, then maybe he had shot somebody. Still, there was no blood at all to indicate that *anyone* was shot.

That was when I saw the holes in the wall, and that was when I remembered what Hardin had said about the man in the next room.

I left his room and walked down the hall to the next one. The door was ajar there, and when I walked in I found out where the two slugs that had been fired had gone.

One was in the left-hand wall and one was in the man on the bed, which was against the right-hand wall—the one between this room and Hardin's.

I heard footsteps out in the hall and Bill came running in with his .32 in his hand. "What happened?" he demanded.

"It's your friend, Wes Hardin."

He looked around. "What about him?"

I pointed to the man on the bed. "He just shot a man for snoring."

24

What had happened was obvious, considering the statement that Hardin had made to me earlier that day.

Apparently the man in the next room was a loud snorer, and Hardin had taken all he could. He fired two shots into the room through the wall, one of which killed the man and stopped his snoring forever.

"I told you he was a killer," I said to Bill. "Now I guess we know he's crazy, too."

"Shit," was all Bill would say, holstering his gun.

He looked around the room some, then turned and walked out. I followed him down the hall to Hardin's room. Some of the other people on the floor had finally gotten brave enough to come out of their rooms.

"Go back to sleep, folks," I told them. "There's nothing to see."

Bill walked into Hardin's room and looked around.

"He took off, Bill. His gear's gone, and so's he."

"Damn," he snapped.

"You'll have to look for him and bring him back," I commented.

"I know my job," he replied wearily. "I'll take Carson and look around. Somebody else might just shoot him."

"Or get shot," I offered.

He nodded, looking depressed.

"Why don't you take Mike instead of Carson," I suggested.

He looked at me for a few moments, either pondering my suggestion or thinking about something else entirely. Then he nodded.

"We'll start out in the morning," he told me.

I was about to suggest he start now, but then I realized that if he was having trouble with his eyes, he'd have trouble seeing in the dark. That must have been why he was having Williams and Carson patrol the streets while he stayed in the brightly lit Alamo.

"Okay, Bill. I'll have the undertaker come and remove the body."

"Okay," he agreed. "You know where I'll be."

"Yeah."

We both left and I shut the door. There were a couple of people peeking into the other room, so I went over and shut the door.

"Go back to sleep," I told them.

I went downstairs and to the front desk to talk to Allie.

"What happened, Clint?"

"Two vacancies just opened up, sweetheart," I told her, and I told her which rooms. "The undertaker should be over in a while to clear the body out. I'm going to wake him up now."

She looked up at approximately where the body was lying and shivered involuntarily.

I touched her shoulder and said: "Why don't you let Homer take over the desk until the body is removed."

She shook her head saying, "It bothers him more than it bothers me. I'll be fine."

I started for the door and she called me back.

"What will you do after you wake the undertaker?"

I thought about Nell, waiting for me at the Alamo, but even she would have to wait a little bit longer.

"I'm going to look around town a bit," I told her. "Hardin may still be here."

I walked over to the undertaker's. He didn't appreciate being woken up, but he said he'd round up some help and move the body.

I started patrolling the town, checking darkened corners and doorways. If Hardin was still in Abilene I might be able to take him into custody. The way Bill's eyes were, if I could keep him from having to face Hardin, in daylight or darkness, I'd feel a whole lot better.

I'd worked my way through town with no luck, and there was only one place left to look—the livery stable.

As I approached the livery I was struck by a gut feeling that Hardin was inside. Over the years I had come to trust my instincts. My first thought was to draw my gun before I entered. But if he was in there that might cause him to shoot me on sight, so I left my gun in my holster and tried the front doors; they were locked. I walked around to the back doors, and they were also locked. I circled the entire structure once and found what I was looking for. There was one small door that had apparently been forced at one time or another. Hardin might have used it to get in. I listened for a few moments, but I couldn't hear anything but the noise the horses were making. I eased the door open enough to accommodate my body and slipped in, pulling the door shut behind me.

I stayed just inside the door for a few moments, letting my eyes adjust to the darkness. Gradually I was able to make out shapes, and then I began to be able to identify them. Once I was able to see, I made my way to Duke's stall. The big horse's instincts were almost infallible—and that's what I would use to determine if there was anyone else inside.

When I reached Duke I put my hand on his neck to let him know it was me, although his nose would have picked up my scent long before. He was slightly on the muscle, which practically assured me of the fact that someone else was in the livery with us. I eased myself out of Duke's stall and crouched down.

"Hardin," I called out, "I know you're in here."

No answer.

"Come on out, Wes, there's no place to go."

Still no answer.

"Son, it'll be a lot easier for both of us if you just give yourself up."

There was still no answer, but I thought I heard the scrape of someone's foot on the floor. I listened intently, trying to locate him before he located me. Suddenly I heard the familiar sound of a match being struck on a boot and then the flame flared up and lit the interior.

Hardin was standing there, match in hand, and he opened a lamp and lit it, brightening the inside of the livery considerably. He carefully blew out the match and then dropped it to the floor.

He must have fled from his room in a big hurry, judging from his disheveled appearance. As I watched he tucked his shirt into his pants and ran his hands through his hair, neatening his appearance. His hands were empty, and both of his Colts were holstered.

"I figured if somebody came looking for me it would be you," he said.

"How's that?" I asked.

"You've got the look," he told me. "When you put on a tin star, you mean to do the job. I've seen the look before, but not very often. Most lawmen I've known have been after whatever they could get."

"Maybe that's why I took the star off a couple of years ago," I said, more to myself than to him.

"You've got it on now, though," he pointed out.

I looked down at the damned thing and then said, "Yep, it seems that way."

"That means you ain't about to just let me ride out of here," he reasoned.

"I can't, Wes," I told him.

"Well, I heard you were good with a gun, I guess we're about to find out how good," he told me.

"I heard you were good too, Wes," I told him. "Too good for me to play games with." What I meant was, he was too good for me to try anything fancy, like hitting him in the hand or the arm. "I'm going to have to kill you, Wes."

He smiled then, his killer's smile with that killer's glint in his eye.

"Confidence, too. I like that. Any time you feel lucky, Mr. Gunsmith."

I didn't feel particularly lucky, but I didn't feel scared, either. I didn't feel apprehensive; I didn't feel elated; I didn't feel anything. I felt as if the whole thing were happening in a vacuum. I imagined it was virtually the first time that either one of us had faced someone when we weren't at least reasonably sure of what the outcome was going to be.

"This is the way you want it, Wes, not me," I told him. "The first move is all yours."

25

"Both of you freeze," a voice commanded from the shadows.

We both did just that and looked in the direction of the voice. Wild Bill Hickok stepped into the light, squinting his eyes slightly. He held his .32 in his hand, pointing somewhere between the two of us.

"Saddle up, Wes, and ride out of here."

"Sure thing, Bill," Hardin said with his eyes still on me. "You're the law."

"Bill—"

"Wait a while, Clint," he told me.

We both watched as Hardin saddled his horse and got his gear together.

"Door's locked, Bill," he said.

"I unlocked it before I came in, Wes. The back one," Bill said.

Hardin nodded and walked to the doors. He found them unlocked as Bill had said and swung them wide. Then he mounted up and rode out without another word to either one of us.

When he was gone Bill holstered his gun.

"It would have been interesting to see who came

out on top," he told me.

"If you could see it," I commented. He stiffened slightly and walked closer to me.

"What do you mean by that?" he demanded.

"First let's talk about why you let him go, Bill," I told him.

He shrugged. "He'll get it sooner or later. We all will, but he's only seventeen. I'd rather he got it later, and somewhere else."

"He's a killer, Bill."

"I know, I know. Clint, you may want to take that badge off because of this, but I'm askin' you not to. I'm askin' you to stay on until this thing is all over with."

"A few more days, right?" I asked.

"That's all it should be," he said. "I'll never ask another favor from you, Clint. I swear."

I waved a hand at him in annoyance and said, "I'll stay."

He smiled and said, "Good," and started to turn away.

"Let's talk about your eyes, Bill." He stopped short and turned half around, not looking at me.

"What about them?" he asked over his right shoulder.

"How long have they been bothering you?"

"Who says they're bothering me?" he asked.

"Come on, Bill. I'm not—" I had been about to say that I wasn't blind. "You have trouble seeing the cards across the table from you. Hell, part of the time you can't even make out your own cards. You're careful not to go out at night, when it's dark. You—"

He held up his right hand and said, "That's enough."

"Talk to me, Bill," I told him. "I'm your friend."

"Yes," he agreed, turning to face me, "you are my friend. One of the few friends I got."

He paced around a bit, then set himself down heavily on a bale of hay.

"It's been a few months, I guess," he said finally. "Before I came to Abilene, anyway. At first it was just a kind of blurriness," he explained, waving a hand in front of his eyes, "when things were far away, you know? Then it started to happen even close up. At night it's worse. You know how it is when you've got a reputation like mine—hell, like yours, too—this is the worst thing that can happen." He looked up at me and added, "I might not even see the shot that kills me."

"So what are you trying to do, then?" I demanded. "Get killed here in Abilene? You trying to make sure you see the shot that kills you? Dammit, Bill." I lowered my voice and asked, "Have you at least seen a doctor?"

"No doctor," he said firmly. "If I go to a doctor word might get around. Every gunny with a hankerin' for a reputation would be lookin' to take me on."

He was right about that, but still, maybe it could be treated.

He stood erect and said, "I don't want to talk about it."

"Why don't you go get some sleep?" I asked him.

"I'll be over at the Alamo, Clint."

I watched him walk out, wondering how I would feel if I thought I was going blind.

I decided to go over to the Alamo, too. I had a sudden urge to get stone drunk!

26

I had a hell of a night.

I'd gotten roaring drunk in the Alamo, and then Nell steered me up to her room, but couldn't persuade me to leave my bottle behind. By morning we were both totally exhausted, and I was hung over to boot. The first time I woke up she was still in bed with me. In fact, she was lying across my chest.

The second time I woke up I could smell coffee. When I opened my eyes Nell was sitting in a chair, wearing a frilly robe and drinking coffee.

"Well, good afternoon," she greeted me when she noticed my eyes were open.

"Oh," I moaned, "what a lousy thing to say to a dying man." Then what she said hit me, and I asked, "Did you say 'afternoon'?"

"I did, and that's what it is. I brought you a pot of strong coffee."

"Pour me a cup, will you?" I asked.

"Yes, sir."

She stood up and then winced, putting her hand to her crotch. "Ouch, I'm going to be sore for days," she told me. Then, smiling lewdly, she added, "Front and back."

Now that she mentioned it, I also felt a soreness between my legs. "I know what you mean," I told her.

She brought me a cup of coffee and I sat up in bed to take it. She was right—it was strong and scalding hot. It peeled a layer of skin from the roof of my mouth.

"You must have had something heavy on your mind last night," she told me.

"Why's that?"

"I've never had to beg a man to come up with me before," she told me. "I couldn't get you away from the bar, and then even after you agreed to come up you had to bring a bottle with you. You paid more attention to that bottle than you did to me, until it was empty," she added, looking hurt.

"I'm sorry," I apologized. "When I'm drunk I get my priorities mixed up."

"What set you off, anyway?" she asked.

I put the empty coffee cup down on her night table and said, "Bad news about a friend."

"What kind of bad news?"

"I'd rather not say. How about another cup of that coffee?"

"You men think wearing a girl out makes her your maid."

"Please," I added.

She smiled and said, "That's more like it."

She brought me the second cup and I drank that one sitting up, my feet on the floor. When I finished I put the cup aside and began looking around for my clothes.

"They're scattered around," she told me. "You threw your pants out the window, but I had one of the girls go down and get them. I even had her clean them."

I looked over at her. Even the morning after, when I was hung over and she was slightly rumpled, she was still one of the most beautiful women I'd ever seen. I told her so.

"Well, thank you," she replied. "It's nice to see that even a hangover can't affect your gallantry."

"Gallant to the end," I told her, pulling my pants on.

"Would you like some breakfast?" she asked, "or some lunch?"

I made a rude face. "I don't think I'll eat anything, ever again."

She gave me another lewd look and said, "I certainly hope that isn't true."

I was so out of it that it took me a few minutes to get her meaning.

"You have no shame, woman," I scolded her, standing up and putting my gunbelt on.

"You'd know that better than anyone," she commented.

I went over to her and kissed her on the forehead.

"What's that for?" she asked, surprised.

"That's for being here when I needed you," I told her.

She touched my face and said, "Well, I'll be here if you need me again."

"Thanks, Nell. I'll see you later."

I left her room and tried negotiating the stairs without falling down. When I got outside the sunlight hit me like a punch between the eyes and I staggered. Then I remembered about Bill's eyes and I was grateful for the fact that I could still be staggered by the brightness of the sun.

Some of us wouldn't always be that lucky.

27

That day three Texas cowboys tried to break Whit Landon out of jail, and I believed that they did so without Phil Coe's knowledge or consent.

For one thing, Bill had left town with Mike Williams, supposedly to hunt for Wes Hardin. I figured Bill only did it for show, so the town council would think that he was after Hardin for killing the man in the next room—who turned out to be a drummer. Coe would never have okayed an attempt on the jail while Hickok was out of town. His whole aim was to embarrass Bill into leaving, or get him fired or, better yet, get him killed. None of this could be achieved while he was out of town.

So the three cowhands, liquored up and acting on their own, decided to break Landon out.

I went over to the jail after leaving Nell, and that was when Tom Carson told me that Bill had taken Mike Williams and gone hunting for Hardin.

"When did they leave?" I asked Carson.

"Early, at first light. I heard that young killer shot a man for snoring. That true?"

"Appears so."

He shook his head in wonder. "I've known a lot of

reasons to kill a body," he said, "but never for snor-ing."

"Apparently, Hardin valued a night's sleep over a man's life."

"Crazy," he said.

"I'm going to get some coffee," I told him. "Want any?"

He looked at me in surprise, and I was kind of sur-prised myself that I was offering, but he said yes and I told him I'd bring back a pot and drink it with him.

When I returned he had two cups on the table and we filled them with strong, black coffee.

"What're you tryin' to do?" he asked as I seated myself. "Soften me up?"

"Soften you up for what, Tom?" I asked innocent-ly.

"You're tryin' to get me to admit I work for Coe," he said.

"I'm just having some coffee to cure a hangover," I told him. "I tied on a beauty last night."

"I hear you been making the acquaintance of Nell Virdon pretty regular," he commented.

"I'd say I know her better than most," I answered.

"She's some woman," he said.

"That she is," I agreed. "She doesn't go in for your kind of fun, though," I added.

He stiffened. "I don't bother you about the way you get your pleasure, Adams, so don't be bothering me about mine."

"I just can't see how a man could get pleasure from beating up a woman."

"That's all they're good for," he replied. "They're all just like my mother used to be," he went on, then stopped himself short when he realized what he was saying. He leaned back in his chair then and said,

"Just never you mind about how I get my pleasure."

He poured himself a cup of coffee, pointedly avoiding to ask me if I wanted some more. I leaned forward and poured myself another cup.

Sitting back in my chair I asked him, "Why'd you sign on as a deputy, anyway?"

"I needed the fifty a month."

"You could have worked for Coe for a lot more," I told him. Coe probably was paying his men nigh onto what Bill was making as marshal, which was a hundred and fifty a month.

"I didn't—" he began, then stopped again. "You think you're so smart," he told me, sneering. "Just so happens I didn't want to work for Coe."

I nodded, wondering how much longer he could go without slipping up. "Where you from, Tom?" I asked him.

He narrowed his eyes at me and snapped, "Well, it ain't Texas, that's for sure."

I was about to remark on that when a voice called out from outside on the street.

"Hello the jail!" a man called.

"What the hell?" Tom said, rising to his feet. He walked to the window with a hand on his six-gun.

"Three men," he announced.

I got up and looked out the window, too. There were three of them, all right, and they were weaving a bit, as if they had been drinking all morning.

"Well, let's see what they want," I suggested. He nodded and pulled his gun out. "Put that away," I told him. "They see that and there might be unnecessary shooting."

He glowered at me, but holstered his gun. I opened the door and we both stepped outside.

"What can we do for you?" I asked.

The spokesman stepped forward, a slightly built man in his early or mid-forties. He spoke with his hand on his gun. "We want you to let that good ole Texas boy outta that cell, hear?" he said.

"Yeah," the other two chorused.

"You fellas started your drinking a little early, didn't you?" I asked them.

"When we drink is none of your business," the spokesman announced. "We're Texans, we can hold our liquor. Now, you just let that good ole boy out if you know what's goo—what's good for—for you," he ordered drunkenly.

I had no doubt that if any one of them drew his gun I'd be able to stop him without killing him. If all three of them drew, I might not get a chance to be that choosy about where I shot.

"Boys, now I'm giving you good advice, and I'd take it if I was you. Sober up, then come on back and talk, if you like. The shape you're in now—"

The man in front waved a hand at me violently and said, "If'n you don't open that cell door now, we're gonna have ta start shootin'," he announced.

I said: "That'd be a down right shame, fellas, because one or all of you might end up getting yourselves hurt."

They all went for their irons at the same time, and I cursed their drunken timing, but there was nothing else I could do.

I drew my gun and shot the first man square in the chest, knocking him over backwards. I moved my aim quickly to the man on his right and shot him in the same place, with the same result. The third man was so scared he fell to his knees as I fired, and my slug caught him in the middle of his forehead.

It was over in seconds, the three of them sprawled in the street, dead.

I turned my head to look at Tom Carson, and he was staring at me with his mouth open and his revolver half out of his holster.

"You didn't fire," I spat accusingly.

He was still staring at me and he jumped when I spoke to him. "I didn't get a chance," he said. He pushed his gun back into his holster and stared at me again.

"I ain't never seen nobody pull a six-gun that fast," he told me, a touch of awe in his tone. "I didn't even get a chance to clear leather."

I ejected the empty shells from my gun and replaced them with live rounds, then put the gun back in my holster.

"Maybe you're just slow," I drawled, stepping off the boardwalk to check the three men out, even though I knew they were dead.

"I'm a pretty fair hand with a gun, Adams," he told me from behind, "and I'm tellin' you I ain't never seen nothin' that fast."

"You've never seen Bill Hickok draw, then."

"Can't be as fast as what I just seen," he said.

I ignored his remark. "We better get the undertaker over here. You go back inside, these three might have friends."

He stood there, still staring at me and I snapped, "Well go ahead!"

He jumped and then hurried back inside, stealing one last glance at me before he closed the door.

I didn't know what was worse, having him hate me or fear me.

I went over to get the undertaker, and again I had to wake him up. Seems he'd been late getting back to bed after I woke him up during the night. When I told him I had three more corpses for him his eyes went skyward, seeking guidance I suppose, and then he told me he'd be right along with some help.

When I got back to the marshal's office I found a surprise waiting for me: Phil Coe was sitting in the chair I'd only recently vacated. When I walked in he and Carson both tried to look very innocent, but I knew I'd interrupted a private conversation.

"Well, Mr. Coe," I greeted him. "Did you come to see the results of your handiwork?"

"What are you talking about?" he demanded, getting to his feet. He had his best gambler's suit on today, complete with watch chain, vest and bowler hat —very dapper.

"You've been inciting these Texas cowboys for a long time, Coe, so today three of them got big ideas, and got killed for it."

"You killed them!" he shot back.

"They wouldn't have been out there waving guns, forcing me to kill them if they hadn't been listening to you," I answered.

He looked at Carson helplessly, then back at me, trying to think of something to say.

Finally unfreezing his tongue he shouted, "I came over here to tell you that I had no knowledge of what those men were going to attempt, Adams, but now you can go straight to hell! I wish they'd killed you!"

"You'll have to get yourself better men than those —and your bushwhackers from the other night—if that's what you're after," I advised him.

"I'll get men," he told me, jabbing the air with his forefinger. "I'll get so many men you won't be able to —to—" He was so angry he was sputtering. "Damn you, Adams, you and Hickok both!" he finally yelled and stormed out of the office.

"What were you and your boss talking about when I came in, Carson?" I asked.

"We weren't talking about nothin'. Hey, I told you," he corrected himself, "he ain't my boss. He was tellin' me just what he told you—that he had nothing to do with those men."

"Except for filling their heads with ideas, and with whiskey courage," I added.

I looked out the window and saw the undertaker with some townspeople, moving the bodies over to his office.

"I get the feeling there's going to be a lot more bodies before this is over," I said.

28

When Bill and Mike came back it was evening and I was in the office, having relieved Carson so he could go and have dinner.

"Anything?" I asked as they walked in, for Mike Williams's benefit. I didn't think Bill would have told Mike what happened the night before.

"No, nothing," Mike told me, tiredly. "He must be halfway back to Texas by now. He got a big head start on us."

Bill looked at me but said nothing.

"Mike, why don't you go and get something to eat," he suggested.

"Sure, Bill. I'll see you later, Clint." Mike left the office. I had the feeling that if Bill had said to him, "Mike, why don't you put your gun in your mouth and pull the trigger," his answer would still have been, "Sure Bill."

When he was gone I said, "You didn't tell him, did you."

"No. Where's Carson?"

"I let him go to dinner."

"Any excitement?"

"Funny you should ask," I replied, and told him what had happened.

"Did you believe Coe?"

"His anger seemed real, and I didn't believe him at first, but after thinking back I'd say yes, I do believe him."

I explained my thinking to Bill about how the clumsy break-out attempt could not serve Coe's purpose while he, Bill, was out of town.

"That makes sense," he agreed.

"Bill, why don't you get some rest?" I suggested as he slumped into the chair in front of his desk.

"Maybe I will," he said, rubbing one hand over his face. "Tomorrow's gonna be busy. The cattlemen should really start flocking in, because the fair opens the following day."

"I wish we had a few more deputies for this fair," I told him.

Standing up he said, "Why don't you give it a shot? Go around and see if you can get anyone. I'll be in my room at the hotel." He wasn't staying at the American House, he was at one of the smaller hotels. He maintained a room there, but he spent very little time in it. "I'll have the clerk wake me up in a couple of hours."

"Okay, I'll see you later."

I thought I'd take his last suggestion to heart and go on kind of a recruitment drive. I was sure there must be a few men in town who could use fifty dollars a month.

It didn't take me long to find out how wrong I was.

Even the men who weren't Texans, and weren't under Phil Coe's spell, were not willing to side with Bill Hickok against "all of Texas."

The consensus of opinion seemed to be that he had picked that fight himself, so now let him finish it.

When I found Bill at the Alamo, I told him that I couldn't find anyone willing to put on a badge.

"I'm not surprised," he said. "We'll just have to handle it ourselves."

Later on I found myself sitting in the jailhouse with Mike Williams, cleaning my gun.

"Don't you have to break it down to clean it?" he asked me.

I showed him the gun and explained how I had modified it. Basically it was a Colt, but where the Colt was a single-action gun that broke down into pieces, mine was a double-action which didn't necessarily have to be cocked to be fired, the way a single-action did. And it was also a solid body.

"If I'm looking for accuracy," I told him, "I'll still cock it to fire, but if I'm looking for speed over accuracy, all I have to do is pull the trigger."

"I see. And you modified the gun yourself?"

"Yes."

"I wondered why Bill called you The Gunsmith. He tells me you may be the fastest man with a gun he's ever seen."

"I'm sure there's faster," I told him.

"Like who?"

"Bill himself, for one. After that—oh, probably Ben Thompson."

"What about Hardin?"

I didn't tell him that we almost found that out last night.

"I've never seen him in action," I said instead. "I've only heard that he's good."

"Anyone else?"

"There's a youngster named Bill Longley who's supposed to be pretty good, but I haven't seen him either. Clay Allison is good also, and I've met him,

but I don't know if he's faster than me. I don't usually talk about it—it's not something I think about a
lot."

I had never set out to become good with a gun or
build a reputation. Being able to shoot fairly straight
was an ability I seemed to be born with. Having been
a lawman, it was inevitable that I would have to use
that talent from time to time to enforce the law, and
being a good gunfighter was liable to get you more
attention in the West than being a good lawman. It
wasn't something I agreed with, but it was something
that could not be ignored.

"I don't know if I could hit that wall with a six-
gun," Mike told me, pointing. "That's why I use the
shotgun." He picked up his weapon, which was a Rem-
ington ten-gauge with twin 28-inch barrels, that
could cut a man in half or blow his head off. You
didn't have to be good with a gun to hit what you
were aiming at with a shotgun, because a shotgun
fired a concentration of metal pellets. The further
they traveled, the wider they spread, until eventually,
at great distances, they became ineffective.

I finished cleaning my gun and put it back in my
holster.

"What made you sign on as a deputy, Mike?"

"I believe in the law, I guess," he answered. "I believe somebody has to uphold it."

It was a better reason than most.

I stood up, picking up my hat, and said, "I think
I'll walk around town a little. Can I bring you anything when I come back?"

He shook his head. "I'm fine, thanks."

I walked the length of Texas Street on one side, and
then came back on the other. There seemed to be increased noise and activity coming from the Bull's

Head Saloon, which led me to believe that some of the cowhands were coming in early for the fair, and they were patronizing the Bull's Head over the Alamo.

When I stopped into the Alamo it was quieter than I had ever seen it at that time of night.

I went up to Roy the bartender and ordered a beer. When he brought it I said, "Kind of dead in here, isn't it?"

"All the Texans are at the Bull's Head," he told me. "We've got some Kansans, Oklahomans, Missourians, Montanans and a few others, but all together they don't make up half the Texans we've got in town."

"I think you're right," I said, sipping my beer. "Where's Nell tonight?"

"Upstairs," he said. Then he added, "Recuperating."

I gave him a meaningful glare and then walked over to the poker tables. There were empty seats at each table, which was in itself unusual. What was also unusual was that Bill seemed to be losing. Just while I was standing there he miscalled a hand, something I had never seen him do. He looked up at me, rubbed his eyes, then looked at the dealer and snapped, "Deal!"

I decided not to watch anymore and walked back to the bar.

"Uh-oh," Roy said, and I looked at him and saw that he was looking at the front door.

Four . . . five . . . six men, dressed in old trail clothes, came walking in through the front doors. The first thing I checked was their guns, all of which were worn high and loose. Obviously not gunhands. Equally obvious was the fact that they *were* trailhands, and probably Texans at that.

What were they doing at the Alamo?

They all lined up at the bar to my left and ordered beers. Roy gave me a look, then went to bring them their drinks.

I turned to take a look at Bill, but all he seemed interested in were his cards. These men may not have been gunhands, but they smelled like trouble.

When he had set up their beers, Roy moved to the opposite end of the bar. I began to nurse my beer, keeping a wary eye on the six cowboys.

They were all rather tall and on the husky side, as if they had been hand-picked for this job because they were the same size. Tall, powerful. . .

Then it hit me, just as it hit another cowpoke who was going to the bar for a drink. He accidentally nudged one of the big Texans and the man turned, hauled off and hit him in the jaw, knocking him backwards until he sprawled across a faro table. Two of the players looked up angrily, saw the six Texans standing at the bar laughing, and the battle was on.

That's why the six of them were so big. They were sent over to the Alamo to start a fight and, in the process, to break the place up.

As the two faro players approached the Texans I started to draw my gun to nip things in the bud, but somebody else wanted a piece of Texas and plowed into me in the process. My gun went flying from my hand and landed behind the bar.

I grabbed up my empty mug, stepped over and brought it down on the head of one of the Texans, knocking him cold, if not killing him. The other five met the charge of the faro players and drove them back with massive fists. Two of them turned to face me and saw what I'd done to their comrade.

"A deputy," one of them said happily, and they advanced on me. Suddenly a bottle of whiskey shattered over one of their heads, courtesy of Roy. I ducked the right hand of the other one and threw a left of my own that landed on his chin. Big as these men were, they were not as large as Moose the foreman had been, and after him anybody else seemed small.

After that it was pure confusion. I couldn't tell who was punching whom, but somewhere in the middle I saw Bill Hickok flailing away. I decided to crawl over the bar to look for my gun, but as I did I was grabbed from behind, dragged off the bar and thrown across the room. I landed on one of the poker tables, and one leg broke—on the table, I mean. I slid off it to the floor and started to get up when I saw a whiskey bottle flying my way. I ducked and the bottle smashed against the wall, showering me with rotgut whiskey. I was glad it wasn't the good stuff.

When I finally made it to my feet I saw one of the Texans take a right on the chin from Bill and start staggering my way. I caught him by the shoulders, turned him around and hit him with my right. Bill gave me a wave and caught a left that made me flinch. I didn't see what happened to him after that because he went down into a pile of bodies.

Damage to Nell's place had been kept to a minimum up to that point, and I knew I'd have to stop the battle before the place really got wrecked. Then I saw Nell coming down the stairs, looking regal in a shimmering blue gown, and carrying a Greener shotgun.

"Nell!" I shouted.

She tried to locate me, and when she did she threw the shotgun to me. Several other hands tried to grab it on the way over, but I caught it successfully and let one barrel go into the ceiling.

The silence that followed was deafening.

"That's it, everyone!" I yelled. "The fight's over."

Men dragged themselves up off the floor, wiping blood from their faces. The six Texans who started things seemed a little worse for wear. As big as they were, they had been outnumbered. The one I'd hit with the beer mug was still sprawled on the floor.

"Roy," I called out, "find my gun back there."

He looked around some, found it and tossed it over to me. With my gun in one hand and the Greener in the other I told the Texans, "Pick up your friend and get moving."

Bill was standing tall, a slight bruise beneath his right eye, but he added, "Tell Coe it didn't work. I see any one of you men in town after this, I'll shoot your ears off. Now git!"

They picked up their unconscious friend and carried him out the doors.

"How about we clean this place up some, men!" I shouted.

Immediately they began to right the tables and pick up chips and cards. Nell came down off the steps and surveyed the damage.

"Well, I guess it could have been worse," she said.

"No, it couldn't," Bill told her, scanning the floor.

"What are you looking for?" I asked him.

"I'm looking for the hand I had when the fight started," he told me. He looked at both of us, who were staring at him, and added, "Well, dammit, I had a full house!"

29

Everything at the Alamo got back to normal surprisingly, and before long the games were back under way. Bill never did get his full house back, but the interruption seemed to do him some good, because his luck changed after that.

I left after that and went over to see the doctor, because the cut on my cheek had been reopened.

The doctor's name was Evans, and he applied some antiseptic to the cut.

"If I had seen you earlier I would have stitched it up, so it would heal without a scar."

"I don't mind another scar, Doc," I told him. He put a piece of tape over it and then probed my ribs and agreed that there didn't seem to be any broken.

"I'm glad you stopped over here, Mr. Adams. I've been meaning to talk to you—that is, the town council has. As a member of the council, I'll take it upon myself to speak to you now."

"About what, Doc?"

"About Marshal Hickok," he answered. "We on the council do not feel that it is in our best interest—the town's best interest—that Hickok continue as our marshal."

"Why is that?" I asked.

"We don't approve of the way he has been handling matters, most notably the problem with Mr. Coe of the Bull's Head Saloon. Marshal Hickok seems to have launched a personal vendetta against Mr. Coe and, as I stated before, we do not feel that this is in Abilene's best interests."

"Why are you telling me all of this, Doctor?"

"Would you like a brandy?" he asked, pouring himself a drink from a crystal decanter. I said I would. I wondered what a well educated man like Evans was doing with a practice in one of the West's wildest towns. I would have expected to see him somewhere like San Francisco, or Sacramento.

He handed me a glass of brandy and then continued. "We understand you have a reputation as a lawman, Mr. Adams. We realize, of course, that you also have a reputation as a gunman, but not as a killer."

"And Bill Hickok is a killer?" I asked.

"You must admit the bulk of his fame rests on his abilities with a gun, not as a lawman. You, on the other hand—"

"Could we get right to the point, Doctor?" I requested.

He frowned at being interrupted, then said, "Very well. We would like you to take over as marshal of Abilene, Mr. Adams."

"And if I say no?"

"Well, we'll have to get someone else. It will take some time, and Hickok will continue as marshal until we find a new man. That is why we'd like you to take the job, so that we can replace Hickok as soon as possible."

I drank the brandy and set the crystal glass down. "Doctor, I thank you for your treatment, and for your brandy, but I will not accept your offer. Bill Hickok is my friend. It's that simple."

"I understand, Mr. Adams, and I respect your loyalty to your friend. Good night."

"Good night, Doc."

So, the town of Abilene was looking to dump Bill Hickok. Maybe they felt that Phil Coe was more important because his saloon brought more revenue to the town. Or maybe Phil Coe himself had some influence with the council and he was engineering Bill's dismissal.

I decided not to reveal to Bill what the council was planning. At least, not yet. Not until the business with Phil Coe was resolved.

30

The following morning, Hickok called his three deputies together at his office.

"Tomorrow is the fair, boys," he told us. "Somehow, the four of us are going to keep the lid on this town, starting tonight."

"And we're still gonna have a man here to watch the prisoner?" Carson asked.

"That's about the size of it," Bill told him. "If Coe is gonna try breaking his man out, it will have to be either today or tomorrow, while we're busy."

"Coe?" Carson asked. "Why has everybody got it in for Coe?"

We all looked at him, and I said, "Who else would want to break the man out of jail?"

"What about those three jaspers you killed?" Carson asked. "Coe said he had nothing to do with that."

"And you believed him?" Williams asked. He gave a derisive snort and Carson sprang to his feet angrily.

"Look—" he started, but I cut in.

"I believed him," I told Mike. "I think those cowboys got liquored up and acted sooner than Coe wanted. Tonight and tomorrow he's going to have a saloon full of Texans, and he'll have plenty of volunteers to come over here with him and break the jail."

"Listen up," Bill called out. "There's a new law that goes into effect tonight. Anyone firing a shot *in town* will be arrested. I expect each one of you to uphold this law."

"What if the lawbreaker don't want to come peaceable?" Carson asked.

"Then you take him any way you have to," Bill told him. He got up from his desk and said, "Let's get to work. Town should be waking up about now, and it'll stay awake until the day after tomorrow. Carson, you take the first shift in here. Mike, relieve him in four hours."

Williams went out on patrol, and I walked out of the office with Bill.

"Strikes me that you might be wrong about Carson, Clint," he offered when we were outside.

"Why's that?"

"Well, if he was Coe's man, he could have let this feller Landon out a long time ago."

"I don't think Coe's plan is to get his man out," I told him. "He's after *you*, Bill, plain and simple. Having one of his men work for you could only help him."

"I guess," Bill commented. After a few seconds of thought he repeated, "Yeah, I guess. Listen, I'm going over to the Alamo. Walk around town a little, will you? Maybe a show of force will keep the trouble down."

"Sure, Bill," I answered.

Yeah, a show of force. Two deputies, one armed with a shotgun because he couldn't hit the side of a barn with anything else. This town is going to blow wide open between today and tomorrow, I thought. I only hoped we came out of it with a minimum of bodies.

There were banners strung across the street proclaiming October 5 as "Cattleman's Fair" day. Already there were cowboys walking the streets, swigging rotgut straight from the bottle, getting a head start on the celebration.

I headed for the Bull's Head, having it in my mind to let them know about Bill Hickok's "new law." Somebody was bound to make the comment—and I knew it was true—that if we expected to lock up every man who fired a shot during the celebration, we better have a lot of jail space.

Maybe if I passed the word some, we could avoid problems.

But I doubted it.

I found the Bull's Head much busier than it normally was at this time of day. The star on my chest got some mean Texas looks, but for the most part—aside from some muttered comments—they held themselves in check.

"You got a lot of nerve coming in here," the bartender sneered.

"I'm the law, sonny," I told him. "I go anywhere I please."

"You want a beer?" he asked, probably ready to tell me that he wouldn't serve me.

"If I want a beer, I'll go over to the Alamo where they serve beer, and not Texas longhorn piss."

I had spoken louder than I'd intended, because the bartender's attitude had bothered me. I heard chairs scrape against the floor and then a voice asked, "What was that you said about Texas longhorns, friend?"

I turned around and found three cowpokes facing

me, one with his hands tucked into his gunbelt, the other two with their hands hanging loosely by their sides.

"Unless one of you fancies himself a pretty good gunhand, I wouldn't make any sudden moves. It could get all three of you killed."

The man who had spoken took his hands from his belt and held them out in front of him.

"We're not gunhands, deputy, and we're not looking for no gunplay. I just asked you what it was you said about Texas longhorns."

"Not that it's any of your business, friend," I told him, "but what I said was that I would rather drink beer than Texas longhorn piss. Now, if any of you men want to argue with that, I'd have to question your taste in beverages."

Well now, they had to stop and think about that for a spell. If they wanted to argue with me, that would mean admitting that they had tasted Texas longhorn piss—and that they liked it.

"Well," the spokesman finally said, "I don't think there's anything there that we can argue with, is there, boys?"

The other two men agreed with him.

"I guess we'll just sit back down, Deputy," he told me.

"I guess that'd be best, friend," I said. The three of them went back to their table and sat down to finish their drinks. I turned to face the bartender again. He was looking unhappy that the three Texans hadn't cleaned the floor with me.

"Tell your boss there's a new law for the Cattleman's Fair. Anyone caught firing a shot in town will be placed under arrest. Pass that along to your customers, too."

"That's crazy," he told me, then he went and made the remark I knew somebody was going to make that day.

"I agree," I told him when he finished. "But pass it along to Coe anyhow. Tell him we're going to keep an eye on the Bull's Head especially, until the fair is over."

"Harassment," he said.

"Shit, no," I told him, "this just happens to be where most of the cattlemen in town will be." That was almost like paying him and Coe a compliment.

31

It was still early, and since it was only going to get busier, I went to see Allie while I had the time.

"Good morning," I greeted her as she stood behind the desk.

She gave me a kind of funny look as she replied, "Good morning, Clint. I guess you've been kind of busy lately."

I guess even though she didn't expect anything from me, she wasn't above feeling a little neglected.

"Things have been sort of hectic, Allie. I'm sorry if—"

"You don't have to apologize, Clint," she told me. "I'm just being silly."

She wasn't being silly, she was being a young girl who had just recently had her first encounter with sex, and was wondering if the second time would be as good.

"Actually," I told her, "I came over because I'm going to be even busier for the next couple of days, and I thought that if you could get free for a bit we might spend some time together."

"Just give me five minutes," she told me, moving around the desk. "And then come on up."

She blushed at her boldness, but hurried up to her room to get ready. Homer, the clerk who'd been so upset by the shooting the other night, stepped behind the desk.

"Pretty girl," I commented to him.

He looked at me, screwing up his face, and said, "I suppose."

I could never understand a man who didn't love women—all women. I know there are men who simply have no use for women, but men like Homer I understood even less. I couldn't comprehend a man preferring another man over a woman.

When I figured Allie had taken five minutes, I went up and knocked on her door.

She was lying in her bed with the sheet drawn up to her neck. From the outline of her body I could tell that she was naked underneath.

"I'm still a little shy," she explained.

"We'll fix that," I told her.

She had drawn the curtain in the room, but it was still daylight out, and the room was well lit. This would be different for her than it had been the first time. Then it had been dark and everything was done by touch. This time she'd see everything.

Her eyes widened as she watched me undress, and when I dropped my pants they widened even more as she caught sight of my erection.

When I was completely naked I walked to the bed and stood by it, letting her look me over. Tentatively, she reached out a hand and ran it over me until she was stroking my penis.

"It's beautiful," she told me.

"You're beautiful," I replied.

I reached down and grasped the sheet with my right hand, pulling it off of her in one swift movement. She was beautiful, no doubt about that.

Her breasts were round and firm, her skin so fair, her nipples already distended with desire. This was new territory for me, too. I had been as much in the dark as she had last time, speaking literally, so now I took the time to look her over carefully.

There was no swell at all to her belly, it was flat as a board, but soft. She had slim hips and thighs, lovely legs and small feet. I knelt next to the bed and began kissing her breasts, nibbling on her nipples. She caught her breath and took my head in her hands. I kissed both breasts, then began to work my way down, over her rib cage, her belly, down, down. . .

I could smell the scent of her readiness, but I skirted that area with my mouth, working instead on her thighs and her legs, working my way down the right one, and back up the left one, as she moaned and writhed on the bed. She began to perspire and I could taste the saltiness of her. I kissed and licked every inch of her delicious skin, and then finally nestled my face between her thighs.

Her juices tasted sharp and salty and her belly began to tremble as I worked her to a fever pitch. Finally I took her little nub between my lips, rolling it, biting it, until both her legs came up to scissor my head between them and waves of pleasure began to wrack her body.

"Oh, God," she moaned. "Oh, Clint. . ."

I climbed on to the bed with her, intending to enter her, but she said, "No, wait." She propped herself up on her elbow and said, "I want to do the same thing to you, now."

I settled down on my back and she began to kiss my chest, flicking her tongue over my nipples. She worked her way down my belly and mapped out the same course on my body that I had done on hers.

When she finally reached my erection she hesitated slightly, as if afraid it might be too big. She used her tongue at first, running it up and down the length of me, then she opened her mouth and allowed the swollen tip of my phallus to enter. Her eyes widened slightly, but then she began to suck on me, taking more of me in little by little. Soon she was moaning and sucking, using her hands to tickle my testicles and massage the part of me that she couldn't fit into her mouth.

Then with a great gasp, she let me slip from her mouth and whispered, "I want you in me, Clint. I feel like I'm burning up."

I pulled her atop me and, using my hands on her butt, I guided my swollen tip to her wet, warm entrance, and then allowed her to settle down on me, taking the full length of me inside.

"Oh, yes, yes!" she cried, riding me up and down. She braced her hands against my chest and began to move up and down so violently that you could hear the sound as our pelvises met again and again.

I moved my hands up to her breasts, squeezing and fondling them while we moved together. Her mouth was open, her head thrown back, and she surrendered herself totally to the sensations of the act. I had not met many women who were willing to shed their inhibitions in bed, but in Abilene I'd met two, and I was grateful for the opportunity.

"I can feel it starting . . . to . . . to . . . oh!"

Her entire body seemed to shake and she slammed herself down on me violently, grinding our pelvises together, and then I let myself go, emptying my seed inside of her.

I pulled her down so that I could kiss her mouth

and she thrust her tongue into mine, then sucked my tongue into hers and bit it, biting too hard at one point.

"I'm sorry," she whispered. "I got carried away."

"That's all right," I assured her. "A little pain is part of it. You do whatever you want."

"Oh," she groaned aloud, "I want to keep you inside of me and not let you go until you swell up again."

"We can work on that," I told her.

"Oh, could you really?" she asked. "Again?"

"With a girl as beautiful as you, Allie," I told her, "it would be easy."

Actually, it wasn't all that easy, but I wanted this girl to enjoy herself thoroughly, because I didn't know if we would ever get an opportunity to be together again.

I kissed and fondled her, and showed her how to touch me so that I would swell again, and, when she felt me beginning to grow inside of her, her eyes widened and she said, "I can feel it! I can actually feel you growing!"

As I began to achieve full erection again she started grinding herself onto me again and in no time she was riding me just as violently as she had before. If possible the mutual explosion we achieved was even better than the first one.

Exhausted, she slid off of me and stretched out on the bed.

"Does it get better and better, Clint?" she asked. "I mean, each time, is it better than before?"

"No, not always," I told her. "It depends on the person you're with. Sometimes it's better with one person than it is with another."

Looking at the ceiling she brushed her hair out of

her eyes and asked, "How is it with me?"

"It's fine," I told her. "It's beautiful."

"For a beginner?" she asked.

I didn't look at her because I didn't want to embarrass her, but I had the impression she was teasing me, so I smiled when I answered.

"Yeah, for a beginner."

She was silent for so long after that I thought maybe she'd fallen asleep. But then she asked, "How do I compare with Nell Virdon?"

I looked at her then, but she was still staring at the ceiling.

"Where'd you hear about that?"

"Women in this town talk," she told me, "and what they talk about are other women—especially a woman like Nell Virdon."

"Do you know Nell?" I asked.

"Not really. Just to say hello."

"Maybe you should get to know her better. You have a lot in common," I said, stretching a point a bit.

"You mean other than you?"

"Yeah, other than me—and to answer your question, I can't honestly compare you to Nell Virdon in bed. It wouldn't do either one of you justice."

I looked at her again and she turned her gaze on me. "I guess you really are a gentleman, aren't you?"

I rolled over on top of her and said, "Don't you believe it."

32

Since there was going to be a large influx of people into town, that also meant an increase in the number of horses that would have to be put up at the livery.

I left Allie in her room, dressing to go back on duty on the front desk.

As I was about to leave, she asked me: "Can we be together again, Clint? Soon?"

"I don't know what the next couple of days are going to bring, Allie. We'll have to see."

"I guess you'll be leaving soon."

"Pretty soon, ycah, I guess," I told her.

I waited for her to say something else, and when she didn't, I left.

I went over to the livery to check on Duke. Nat, the regular livery man, was there sweeping out some of the stalls.

"Hi, Nat."

"Hello, Clint. I'm just sweeping out some of these stalls. We're gonna be gettin' a lot of animals in here."

"That's what I came over to talk to you about, Nat."

Nat was about fifty-five or so, a dried-out drunk

who had started out sweeping stalls in the livery for the old owner, then became the new owner. He was still sweeping out stalls, but at least he owned them lock, stock and manure.

"What about, Clint?"

"The big fella."

"Duke?" he asked, looking over his shoulder at the big black. "What's the matter? Ain't I taking good care of him?"

"The best, Nat, the best. But with all the horseflesh you're going to have in here, I know you're going to have to double up some."

He held up his hand to stop me. "Say no more, Deputy. I would never make that big beast of yours share a stall with anybody. Besides, if I did he'd probably kill the other animal."

I put my hand on the old man's shoulder and said, "Thanks, Nat."

I turned around to walk out, and that's when I saw them. There were three of them, and they all had their guns out, pointing right at me.

"I told you all we had to do was stake out his horse and he'd show up," the man in the middle told the others.

By now they'd all begun to look alike to me. Trail-worn men wearing filthy clothes.

"You gents looking for me?" I asked.

"That we were, Deputy, and now we found you. Eddie, take care of the old man. We don't want him running for help."

The man on the right, apparently Eddie, moved towards Nat, who was saying, "Hey, what's going on here?" But he was cut off when Eddie pistol-whipped him into unconsciousness.

"If he's hurt bad, you'll pay," I told the man called Eddie.

He laughed, stepped towards me and tapped me over the head with the barrel of his gun. My hat cushioned the blow some, and I didn't really think it was meant to do much more than it did, anyway. It drove me to my knees, and Eddie was able to step in and remove the revolver from my holster. He threw it away. I heard it land, but I didn't see where it had gone.

I turned my head to the left and saw Nat, lying on the ground, bleeding from the head, but he was still breathing.

"Sorry, Nat," I muttered.

He didn't say, "Don't mention it," but I knew he would have if he could.

I think I might have blacked out for a moment, but when I was yanked to my feet I became aware again.

"Eddie, you and Danny work the deputy over some. Coe don't want him dead, he just wants him out of action for a while—like two days."

Two days? I repeated in my head. Two days worth of hurt could find me dead, I wanted to tell them, but I couldn't find my voice.

It was Eddie—or maybe it was Danny—who gave me the first shot. And of all places to pick, he had to hit me in my sore ribs. I folded over and went down on my face.

"Hey, Ace, this guy just folded up from one punch. You sure we got the right guy?" That was Danny—or maybe it was Eddie. Whoever it was, I wanted to answer his question for him. Yes, you've got the wrong guy.

Tell him he's got the wrong guy, Ace.

"Naw, he's the right guy, all right," Ace told him. "He's playin' possum."

One of those two guys bent down and looked me in the face while I was struggling to my knees.

"Is that right, friend? Are you playin' possum?"

Not to make a liar out of Ace, I drove up from the ground as hard as I could and hit him in the face with my right fist.

"Shit!" he snapped, backing up and almost falling. "My nose is bleeding!"

"I told you he was the right guy," Ace gloated.

I finally made it to my feet in time to catch a left fist to my own face, courtesy of—well, one of those guys.

Things got kind of hazy after that. They were beating on me for a while, and then they weren't, but it sounded like they were. I mean, I could still hear the blows being struck, but I didn't feel anything.

I tried opening my eyes and it worked. I was lying on my back in a pile of hay, watching another big, trail-worn man beat up on my three.

When all the activity was over, the big man came over to me. It was then that my eyes focused—though only for a second—and I recognized the giant trail foreman, Moose.

"Hey, friend, you're really a mess," he told me.

I tried to answer him, but all I could do was breathe hard.

"Little out of breath, huh?" he asked. "So are your friends. Hey, you got a doctor in this town?" he asked.

Somehow I managed to tell him that there was a doctor.

"Well then, let's get you and this here old guy over to him. I'll take you first, friend," he told me. He bent over, grabbed my arm and threw me up on his shoulder. The sudden movement caused something to rattle loose in my head. It bounced around for a few seconds, then it must have hit something important, because everything went dark.

33

When I woke up I was in my hotel room, lying on the bed. There were three people in the room with me.

One was Doc Evans, who looked down at me and said, "You got yourself pretty messed up again, Mr. Adams, but you should be all right with some rest and care."

"How did I get here?" I asked.

The second person in the room, Allie, answered that question.

"A big man carried you here," she told me. "I told him to take you to your room and then I sent him for the doctor."

That's when the third person in the room spoke up. Nell Virdon. "I saw him carrying you down the street as if you were a baby," she told me, "and I came to see if you were alive or dead."

Allie and Nell in the same room. It was funny, but that was all I could think about.

It didn't seem to bother either one of the women, both of whom stood nearby and watched as the doctor treated my various cuts and abrasions.

"He'll need some care," Evans said when he had finished.

"We'll take care of that, Doctor," Nell said, and I

saw Allie nod at her in agreement.

"You look like you've got a couple of willing nurses here, Mr. Adams. I'm leaving you in good hands."

With that the doc packed up his little black bag and left me to their care.

I had a headache for most of the day and into the night, and became aware of it only when I was awake. I was in and out most of the time, but either Allie or Nell was there every time I woke up.

Once, during the night, I asked Allie, "Where's Bill?"

"At the Alamo, I guess. He was up here once, but you were asleep."

"Is everything all right?" I asked.

"He told me to tell you that the lid is still on, but that he needs help sittin' on it. What's that mean?" she asked.

"Means I've got to get out of this bed and strap on my—" I stopped and swiveled my head around so fast I almost knocked something loose inside again.

"Careful!" she snapped.

"My gun!" I snapped. "Where's my gun?"

"It's right over there, on the dresser," she told me. "But you ain't gettin' up yet, Clint Adams. At least not until tomorrow some time. It's the middle of the night."

"My revolver," I told her. "Hang it on the bed-post, Allie, like a good girl."

"Only if you promise you won't try to get up."

"I promise, I promise. Now hang it on the post, where I can get to it if I need it."

She went over to the dresser to get my colt, muttering something about men and their guns.

"Sometimes I think men care about their guns

more than they do about women," she remarked, hanging it on the bedpost.

"Honey," I told her," "women keep men happy, but guns keep them alive."

And on that note I drifted off to sleep again.

34

By morning every inch of my body ached, every muscle made its presence known by hurting, yet I felt stronger.

Nell was there when I woke up.

"How do you feel?" she asked.

"I ache, but I feel stronger."

"I brought you some coffee, black and strong," she told me. "Why don't you sit up so you can drink it?"

I pushed myself up to a seated position, and accepted the cup from her.

"It's good," I told her.

"Marshal Hickok wanted me to tell you that when he got to the livery with that big fellow, Moose, the three men were gone."

I nodded, then remembered the livery owner.

"Nat," I said, "how's Nat?"

"He's fine. He's got a headache, but that's the only part of him that hurts. Doc says they must have punched and kicked you everywhere they could, then went back and started over. Thanks to—what was his name, Moose? Thanks to him you're still in one piece."

"Where'd he go?" I asked.

"Once he was sure you were all right, he said he wanted to go and enjoy the fair."

"The fair! It's today!" I snapped.

"It sure is."

I put the cup down and swung my feet to the floor.

"I've got to help Bill."

"Go ahead," she told me, "stand up."

I stood up and all of my muscles screamed out their objections, especially my legs. I sat back down just seconds before I would have fallen down.

Nell laughed. "I'll get you some breakfast. You'll feel stronger after you've eaten." She started for the door, then turned and said, "I'll let Allie bring it up. I've got to get back to the Alamo."

"How are you two getting along, Nell?"

"Fine. Why shouldn't we?" she asked. "Oh, you mean because we've shared you?" Shaking her head, she said, "You men. No, Clint, we're not adversaries. In fact, I think we've become friends, and we'll still be friends, even after you're gone."

"That's good."

"It is. By staying friends, we'll remember you. I'll see you later."

"Tell Bill I'll be down to help him sit on that lid," I said.

Here it was, the day of the fair, and "the lid" was still on the town. Maybe it was a good sign; maybe it would stay that way.

Who was I kidding? If that were the case, why would Coe have sent his three boys to put me out of action for a while? He wanted me out of the way for tonight, the night of the fair. Moose had ruined that for him, though. He'd interrupted things before they could hurt me badly enough to keep me down. After I had something to eat, I'd be on my feet, backing Bill, when the crunch finally came.

And it would come tonight, of that I was sure. What I wasn't sure of was, could Abilene stand it?

It wasn't long before Allie came up carrying a tray of food: eggs, bacon, potatoes, and more strong, black coffee. While waiting, I had finished the first pot.

"How do you feel this mornin'?" she asked, setting the tray down on the night table.

"There's nothing wrong with me that a good breakfast won't cure," I assured her.

She refilled my coffee cup, then took the entire tray and placed it across my lap.

"Actually," I went on, "I feel pretty good. You're a damned fine nurse, Allie. This is the second time you've nursed me back to health."

"I didn't do it alone this time," she corrected me. "Nell did as much work as I did."

"You two been getting along, I see," I commented.

"Very well," she told me. "You were right about our having things in common."

That surprised me. But it confirmed what Nell had told me.

"Good, I'm glad."

She pulled a chair next to the bed and sat by me, watching me eat.

"What have you got on your mind, Allie?" I finally asked.

"Nell told me you want to go out and help the marshal," she said.

"Actually, it's my job. But I'd want to go out and do it anyway. He's my friend, Allie."

"That's important to you, isn't it?" she asked. "That he's your friend, I mean?"

"It's very important," I told her. "I don't have all that many friends."

"That's sad."

"No, it's not really. I travel a lot now. You lose some of the old friends like that, and you don't make very many new ones."

She looked down and then asked, "What about me —and Nell."

I finished the last of the eggs and put the tray aside. Then I touched her cheek and said, "I don't make many new friends, but I remember the ones I do make, Allie. If I don't get a chance to tell that to Nell, would you tell her for me?"

She smiled and took hold of my wrist. "Sure, Clint."

"Now, move back so I can get up."

"Already?"

"No time like the present," I said confidently.

She slid her chair back, and I swung my feet to the floor. I stood up and looked around for my pants. They were on a chair by the window and she got them for me. I staggered a bit trying to get them on, but I finally made it without falling. Next she handed me my shirt, then I sat down and let her help me with my boots.

I took the gunbelt off the bedpost and strapped it on.

"Have you killed many men?" she blurted out suddenly. Then she added quickly, "You don't have to answer that. I—I'm sorry, I didn't mean to ask that."

"Why did you?"

"Well, because I think I've gotten to know you while you've been here. I mean, the real you. You're kind, you're gentle—I *know* how gentle you are—but you have this reputation, and you have friends like—"

"Like Bill Hickok?"

"Yes."

I put my hands on her shoulders and told her, "It's

a fair question, Allie. Yes, I've had to kill men over the years. There have been a lot of years, so there have been a lot of men, but I don't count them. I think I stopped wearing a badge because more and more I found myself upholding the law with my gun. You don't need a badge to use a gun."

"Why didn't you put down your gun instead of your badge?" she asked.

I smiled at her. "That's a naive question, sweetheart. If I put down my gun, whether I keep my star or not, I'll be a dead man so fast it would make your head spin. That's just the way it is."

She put her head against my chest.

"That's sad," she said, for the second time.

I put my arms around her and replied, "I know, honey. But that's how it is."

35

"Onc way or another, you wind up in bed with a pretty girl around," Bill said to me.

"I'd prefer to do it an easier way," I told him, rubbing my sore ribs. "How do things look?"

"Wait until dark," he said.

"I'm going to get a beer."

"Get me one too, will ya?"

We were at the Alamo, and Bill was in his customary spot, with his back to the wall and his hands full of cards.

I went over to Roy and told him to draw me two beers.

"Trying to make up for lost time?" he asked. I grimaced. "How you feeling?"

"Lousy, and things promise to get worse."

"Don't worry," he told me, setting the two beers down. "Promises are made to be broken."

"So are bones," I said. Then I brought the beers over to Bill.

"Empty chair," he invited, pointing across the table.

"Uh-uh," I said. "I like being on my feet again. I'm going to stand for a while."

He laughed and told the dealer, "Go ahead, deal."

I drank my beer and stretched, trying to work the kinks and the aches out.

"I saw Coe over at the general store when I came in, a few minutes ahead of you, Clint," Bill said from behind me. I turned around and looked at him. "He might even still be there."

If I went over there I knew what I'd end up doing. Already I'd taken too many lumps to do anything else. Then again, if I paid him back for the bumps and bruises I had collected by giving him some of the same, Abilene would blow up for sure.

But then, that was already inevitable, wasn't it?

I finished my beer and left the empty mug on the poker table.

"Just don't get killed, huh?" Bill called out. "I'm gonna need you tonight."

If Coe was in the general store, he'd be heading back to the Bull's Head when he was finished. I positioned myself in an alley that he'd have to pass to get there. I kept massaging my sore ribs and feeling the lumps on my face just so I wouldn't change my mind.

When I heard footsteps on the boardwalk I stopped rubbing my ribs and got ready. When he came into view, carrying a small package, I grabbed him and pulled him into the alley.

"What the—"

I pushed him into the alley ahead of me and he dropped his package. It split open, but I couldn't see what was in it, because it was still covered by brown wrapping paper.

"Adams!" he snapped when he recognized me.

"Surprised to see me, Coe?" I asked. I swung my right fist and it connected with his jaw. I felt a satisfying jolt up my arm from it, and he staggered back, his hand going to his face.

"You're crazy!" he shouted, looking at the blood on his hand.

"No, I'm mad," I told him. I stepped in and hit him with my left, which drove him up against the wall.

"Damn you, Adams," he cursed. He launched himself off that wall and threw a punch. I ducked inside and landed two blows to his ribs, both with my right on the same side. I wanted him to feel some of the soreness I felt.

"Ugh!" he groaned as the air was forced out of his lungs.

"Thought your boys had put me out of action for good, didn't you, Coe?" I asked. I hit him with my right, a downward blow as he was bent over, clutching his ribs. It split his cheek and drove him to the ground.

"Well, I'm still up and around, Coe, and I'll be backing Hickok all the way. I want you to remember that."

I balled up both fists, intending to pummel him, but instead I turned and walked away, leaving him on the alley floor, his face bloody from a split lip and a cut cheek. I hoped his ribs hurt like hell, too.

Okay, so I'd felt a certain amount of satisfaction beating him to the ground, but now he probably hated me as much—or more—than he did Bill.

If it came down to gunplay that night, I knew I'd have to kill him, or he'd surely kill me. And I was the one who had wanted to avoid having the Coe-Hickok feud end in gunplay.

There didn't seem to be much chance of that any more. Even if there had been, I'd taken care of it just now. If Coe didn't try and kill Hickok, he was sure to make a try for me.

As I was walking out of the alley I noticed that

package of his on the ground. Apparently he'd kicked it over and the paper had ripped wide open. It was a flowered music box. He'd probably bought it for a ladyfriend, but right now it was playing its sweet lullaby for Phil Coe.

36

Hours later I was walking Texas Street on one side while Mike Williams was patrolling the other. Tom Carson guarded the prisoner, while Bill stayed in the Alamo. It was closing in on dark, and that's when Bill and I figured Phil Coe to make his move.

I stopped into the Alamo and saw Nell Virdon, mixing with the customers a little early. When she saw me she stiffened momentarily, then came over.

"I heard you were up and around," she told me. She was lovely in a gown of pink, cut low over her full breasts, and she wore lip rouge of the same color. "I don't agree with this, you know. You should still be in bed."

"Is that a proposition?" I asked, grinning.

"No, you ass, it's my opinion. If you don't care about my opinion, that's your business," she told me angrily, and stalked off to watch one of the faro games. I wondered what she was upset about.

"Roy, a beer," I ordered from the bartender.

He brought it and told me, "The boss is jumpy tonight. I've never seen her this tense."

I nodded, drinking my beer, wondering what could be making her so nervous. If she was just nervous for

191

me, I could appreciate that, but if it was something else, I wanted to know what.

I finished the beer and said, "I've got to get back out there, Roy. See you later."

I looked over at Bill and he was looking at me, but didn't seem to see me. I wondered if he *could* see me. I decided not to test him, and left without waving.

It was to Bill's disadvantage that Coe was apparently—or obviously now—waiting until after dark to make his play. Did Coe know about Bill's eyes? Had he figured it out the same way I did? Maybe not. I couldn't see Coe getting that close to Bill, especially since Bill knew his eyes were not in good shape. He'd be sure to keep Coe at arm's distance.

When I left the Alamo I waved at Mike Williams and walked down to the livery. I hadn't yet been to see Nat, the livery man who'd been pistol-whipped the day before.

"How you doing, Nat?" I asked him as I entered. The place was jam-packed with horseflesh, but off in the corner I could see Duke, standing alone and proud in his own stall.

Nat had a bandage on his head, but his spirits were good.

"Take more than a bump on the head to keep me down, Clint."

"Nat, I'm sorry about that. Those men were after me, and you just happened to get in the way."

"Hell, man, don't apologize. It weren't your fault," he assured me. "How you feeling, anyway? Looks like you caught a few bumps and bruises yerself."

"I'm okay, Nat."

"Well, listen here. I got me an old shotgun in the back, there," he told me, pointing. "You need any help, you give me a holler."

I put my hand on his shoulder and said, "Thanks a lot, Nat. I'll remember. How's the big boy?"

"Oh, he's fine. A little crowded in here, but he's pretty much got enough space for himself."

"I appreciate the way you've taken care of him."

"It's been a pleasure to have a horse that beautiful in my barn, Clint."

"Take care, Nat."

"You take care, Deputy. And remember, me and my shotgun are here if ya need us. I'd like me a shot at that yahoo who creased my skull."

"If I see him, I'll give him one for you," I promised on the way out.

My next stop was the marshal's office, as the darkness finally fell. Tom Carson was sitting behind Bill's desk, nervously fiddling with his six-gun. When I walked in, he hurriedly holstered it and put his hands on the desk top.

"What do you want?" he demanded.

"I'm just checking to make sure everything is all right, Carson," I told him. "What are you so jumpy about?"

"I'm not jumpy," he insisted. "It's just this waiting around for something to happen."

"That's called being jumpy," I told him.

"Dammit, Adams!" he snapped, jumping to his feet.

"So is that," I said, and left him there, satisfied to have gotten his goat so easily.

Torches had been set up all along Texas Street, so that the fair could go on even after dark. There had been some sporting activities put on during the day, such as horse races and sharpshooting competitions, but I had not been tempted to compete in either one. I never fired my gun for "fun"; and Duke was my partner who carried me when I needed him. I didn't play with him, either.

Music was filtering out into the streets not only from the two main saloons—the Alamo and the Bull's Head—but from the smaller ones as well. For some reason, the night seemed to have an echoing effect on all of the music, weaving it into one eerie, echoing song.

I was surprised that no arrests had been made for shots being fired in town. I knew there had been shots fired, I had heard them at various times, but perhaps they hadn't been fired by Coe's men, and the culprits had been let off with just a warning. Either that or there just weren't any of us around to make any arrests when the shots were fired.

I positioned myself on the Alamo side of Texas Street, watching the comings and goings of the people involved with the fair; about three out of every four appeared to be cowhands. Whether they were Texans or not could not be told just from the way they looked, but trail-dusty clothes pretty much branded then as cowhands.

Suddenly, I heard some shooting. Not just an odd shot, as I'd been hearing throughout the day—but several shots in succession, obviously fired from different guns.

I ran into the street to try and determine where they were coming from. Mike Williams rushed out also, from the other side.

"Where did it come from?" he asked.

"I couldn't tell," I answered.

We stood still, waiting for more shots to be fired, to give us some indication of where to look.

After a few moments they came, two quick shots from one gun, and then an answering report from a second.

"I think they came from there," Mike said, pointing at the northern end of town.

"If they did, it was from around the corner," I told him.

The livery stable was around the corner.

"Duke," I said.

"What?"

"Come on," I told him, starting off at a run.

I was afraid for Duke. Coe had made several tries on me, and had more or less failed—aside from those bruises. Maybe he'd decided to take it out on me by doing something to Duke.

If I went to the stable and found that any harm had come to the big horse, I knew I wouldn't be able to stop myself from going after Coe and killing him.

"Where are we going?" Mike asked.

"The livery," I told him. Hastily I added, "We'll check and see if old Nat is all right. Maybe he can give us some idea of where the shots came from."

When we came into sight of the livery stable, the front doors were open and Nat was standing in the doorway, with his shotgun.

"Nat," I called, "are you okay?"

"Yeah, I'm fine. I heard them shots, though."

"Duke?"

"The big boy's fine too," he assured me.

"Where'd the shots come from?" Mike asked.

"Near as I can tell somewhere behind the stable," he told us. "I wasn't about to run out the back doors and make a target out of myself."

"Stay here," I told him, "we'll check around back."

As we started around I reminded Mike, "It's going to be dark back there, Mike."

"Right."

When we reached the back of the stable I held my

hand out to slow him down and keep him behind me. I took my gun out now and eased around the corner, ready to hit the dirt if a shot was fired at me.

There was no shot, but I did hear voices, and then the sound of running feet.

"Well, there's somebody back here," I said. "Or at least there was. Let's take it slow, anyway."

We eased around the corner together and we were looking into pitch-black darkness. I closed my eyes, to accustom them to the darkness, and then opened them. I looked around, trying to make out shapes, trying to see if there was somebody lying on the ground either wounded or dead from the shots we had heard.

"Can you make out anything?" he asked.

"No, it looks clear."

We moved into the blackness now, guns ready, and cut across the entire length of the stable without encountering anyone, dead or alive.

"There was somebody back here," I told him. "I heard them."

"They must have slipped out between buildings," he figured.

"Yeah, but why?" I questioned. "And what was the shooting about?"

"Maybe they both ran because they didn't want to be arrested," he suggested.

"Two guys shooting at each other," I told him. "You think they're suddenly going to forget that and run away together?"

He shrugged.

"You slip through there and see if you find anything," I suggested. "I'll go back around front."

"Okay. See you back in front of the Alamo."

"Right."

I went back around the livery, and as I came out into the light Nat was standing there with his old shotgun ready.

"Nat!" I shouted.

"Jesus!" he said, lowering the twin barrels. "You almost got yourself blown from here to hell."

Grateful that he hadn't pulled the triggers, I holstered my gun and said, "Did you see anyone else come around?"

"If I had, *they'd* of got blown all to hell," he assured me.

I believed it.

I put my hands on my hips, annoyed that we hadn't found anything. I wondered what was going on, and then it hit me. I knew why those shots had been fired.

We'd been suckered.

The whole thing had been set up to get us away from Texas Street, away from the Alamo, and away from Bill Hickok.

37

As I realized what they'd done, I heard the gunfire erupting from Texas Street. Hoping I wasn't too late, I started running for all I was worth, knowing that with his limited vision, Bill could step out of the Alamo and not see the shot that killed him.

As I turned the corner into Texas Street I saw a mob of men, half of whom were carrying torches. The street looked almost as well lit as it did during the daytime, which led me to believe that Coe did not know about Bill's eye trouble. If he had, he wouldn't have let any of the men carry a torch.

Instead of working my way through the crowd, which was obviously headed for the Alamo, I got up on the boardwalk and tried to beat them there.

I could hear the shots coming from in front of the mob, and Phil Coe's voice calling, "For Texas!" or something like it. I know he kept yelling "Texas" this and "Texas" that, and the throng of Texans with him cheered every time he said the name of their home state.

I was a couple of doors away from the Alamo when Bill stepped out to meet the mob. I could see Coe as he stopped at the sight of Bill standing in front of the saloon doorway. He held up his hand to quiet the crowd.

I have to admit, Bill cut a pretty impressive figure, standing there in his frock coat and flat-brimmed hat, his arms folded across his chest—which I considered a foolish and unnecessary show of bravado. His hands should have been hanging at his sides, where I noticed he was now wearing both of his .32 pistols. His hair was clean and his mustache neatly trimmed. He looked like he was ready for a church social, not a shootout.

Another thing I could see was that Bill was squinting out over the mob, and I hoped to God he could make out Coe standing right in front.

I decided against going over to stand beside Bill. Instead, I stepped into a shadowy doorway and waited.

"Who fired those shots?" Bill demanded in a loud, authoritative voice.

Coe took a couple of steps forward and said, "We all did, Marshal," with a sneer in his voice.

I could see Coe's face clearly now, carrying the marks from the beating I'd given him. I wished now that I had given him a worse thrashing, something that would have kept him off his feet for days, which is what he had intended for me.

"That's funny, Coe," Bill called out, "you're the only one I see with a gun in his hand."

I doubted he could see even that, but it was a safe assumption to make, since there hadn't been enough shots to indicate more than one person firing.

"We're celebrating, Marshal. There ain't no law against that," Coe shot back.

"There *is* a law against firing your gun in town, Coe. I guess you can consider yourself under arrest."

"You gonna break up our celebration, Marshal? My friends might not like that," Coe pointed out.

"Your friends will like whatever you tell them to like, Coe. Give up your gun and tell them to go back to the Bull's Head for a round of drinks on the house."

Coe shook his head. "No chance, Marshal. We're tired of letting you push good Texans around. You've got one of our men in your jail, and we want him released."

"You're gonna join him there. You're under arrest. Now throw down your gun."

"No chance, Hickok," he said again. "I'll see you dead first."

"That's your choice to make," Bill told him.

Coe had his gun in his hand, and his hand was hanging at his side. He had the advantage in that Bill's guns were still holstered, and Bill's arms were still folded across his chest.

I saw it all as if it were happening in slow motion. First, Bill dropped his hands to his sides, not to draw, but to be ready. Coe misread the move, and began to bring his gun up to fire. I wasn't at all sure that Bill could see Coe's move, but luckily his hearing was un-impaired. Even from where I was—twice as far from Coe as Bill was—the click of Coe's hammer was clearly audible in the silent street.

I watched as Bill's hands streaked to his .32s and drew them simultaneously.

It was one against one, and normally I would never have made a move, since no one in the crowd went for his gun. With Bill's eyes giving him trouble, how-ever—and I had no way of knowing just how bad they were—I couldn't take the chance.

I drew my gun as Bill drew his, and fired just a split

second after he did. The shots were so close together that you couldn't tell that there were two.

My shot hit Coe in the chest, knocking him back, the gun dropping from his hand. I had no idea where Bill's shot had gone at the time, and I couldn't believe that he had missed not only Coe but the *whole crowd* —completely!

Coe fell back into the arms of the man behind him, who jerked away, letting him fall to the ground on his face.

The festive mood of the crowd quickly disintegrated, and no one seemed willing to draw on Bill in defense of Coe, since Coe was already dead.

"You men go back to the Bull's Head," Bill told them. "Drinks are on the house. Go on!"

As the crowd began to disperse, most of them heading for the saloon, I holstered my gun. Bill still had his out. When he heard someone running from the other direction, he turned quickly, ready to fire.

I recognized the running man as Mike Williams, who must have circled all the way around from the livery. He'd obviously heard the shots and was rushing to help.

I realized a split second too late that Bill probably wouldn't recognize Mike as he was coming from out of the darkness into the light, shotgun at the ready. All Bill saw was a figure holding a shotgun.

"Bill!" I shouted, "Don't—"

The sound of his pistol seemed extra loud as he fired. I saw Mike Williams jerk as the slug entered his chest. And then he stopped dead in his tracks, as if he couldn't believe what happened. First the shotgun fell to the ground as he threw his hands up to the wound, trying to stem the flow of the blood, and then he fell forward onto his face. I knew he was dead before I reached him.

I got to him first and turned him over; he wasn't breathing. I heard Bill behind me and glanced up at him. His face looked like it had been carved out of stone as he stared down at the friend he had just killed.

I couldn't stop him, then, as he turned and took off at a dead run. I knew where he was headed and sped after him.

First he stopped at Phil Coe's body and pumped two more bullets into his enemy's corpse. Then he kept on going, heading for the Bull's Head.

When I reached the saloon he was already inside, and the place was emptying out fast.

The bartender who favored foam came running out and told me, "It's Hickok. He's gone crazy. He's bustin' up the place!"

"That's a shame," I told him, and he kept on running.

I stood at the entrance and watched Bill.

He had already kicked the legs out from beneath one of the larger gaming tables, and he was using one of them to destroy the rest of the tables. Then he discarded the leg and picked up a small table top and threw it into the massive mirror behind the bar. After that he drew both his guns and began shooting at anything that was made of glass. He shot out lamps, blew bottles apart, picked off the glasses behind the bar. When he ran out of bullets he calmly reloaded and then continued firing, as if he were in a turkey shoot. He never missed that I could see, and when he was done the place was a shambles. There were rivers of whiskey running along the floor, shards of glass and pieces of broken tables lying all around.

At that point I stepped inside. Bill reloaded, then holstered both his guns and looked up at me coldly.

"Let's go over to the jail," he told me. He walked

past me and I followed in his wake. I pitied poor Tom Carson if he were foolish enough to still be there.

Bill kicked in the door to his office. A startled Carson turned and was even more startled to find Bill standing there. He probably was expecting Coe.

"Where were you while the shooting was going on?" he demanded in a tone so cold it made me shiver.

"I—I was guarding the prisoner," Carson stammered, his eyes reflecting the fear he felt.

"Why are you so surprised to see me, Carson?" Bill asked. "Were you expecting Phil Coe to come over and tell you that I was dead?"

"N-no, Marshal. I swear, I—"

"You stayed to guard the prisoner, huh?"

"That's right."

"Where is he, Carson?" Bill asked, walking to the back where he could see the cells. "Where is he now?"

"He, uh, he—" Carson stammered, his eyes looking at me pleadingly. "He got away!" he shouted, as if it were an inspiration. "That's it, he got away. Some cowboys came over and they—they broke him out. There was n-nothing I could do, Marshal. Honest! You gotta believe me!" Carson pleaded.

"I do, huh?" Bill asked. "I'll tell you what I believe, Carson. I believe that you've been working for Coe this whole time, spying on me. I believe that when you heard the shooting you assumed Coe had killed me and you let the prisoner go." At this point he started walking toward Carson saying, "And I believe that you should be lying dead out in that street, and not my friend Mike Williams!"

Carson took this to mean that Hickok was going to kill him, and he went for his gun. I guess he figured he might as well die with his gun in his hand.

Bill didn't even bother to draw, though. He grabbed Carson's wrist as the frightened deputy came up with his gun and he slammed the wrist down on the desk. I heard the bones crack and Carson screamed in agony, dropping the gun.

"You son of a bitch!" Bill snapped, smashing Carson in the face with his right hand, knocking the man over the desk.

"You bastard!" Bill shouted, rounding the desk and literally jumping on Carson's chest. Carson wanted to scream but the air was gone from his body and he couldn't make a sound.

Shouting more obscenities at the man, Bill pulled him to his feet, ripped the deputy's star from his chest, taking a portion of the shirt with it, and threw him out of the office into the street.

He followed him out, pulled him to his feet and, still shouting at him, pummeled Tom Carson's face into a bloody, unrecognizable mess.

When I felt that Bill had vented enough of his anger on Carson I stepped in and wrapped both of my arms around his chest, pulling him off the semiconscious man.

"That's enough, Bill," was all I said, and it seemed to work.

He was breathing hard, but did not struggle to get away from me. Instead, he grabbed my arms with his hands, holding on tightly and said, "I'm okay. You can let go."

I released him and he just stood there, swaying as if exhausted from his rampage. He turned around and looked at me and I could see the pain in his eyes. "Mike—" he said.

"Go ahead and take care of him, Bill," I told him. "I'll handle everything else."

He stared at me for a moment, then nodded and turned around. He bent, picked up his hat, and walked away.

There had been a small crowd gathered to watch Bill administer the brutal beating, and I pointed to two of them, saying, "You get the doctor, and you get the undertaker. Move! The rest of you go home."

I got down on one knee to check Carson. His wrist was broken, I knew that, and I could see a piece of bone sticking out from where his cheek used to be. If I didn't know it was him, I would never have been able to tell.

The blowup had come and gone, and now all we had to do was wait for the repercussions.

38

The following day Hickok had the Bull's Head boarded up, but I knew that wouldn't last. Turned out I was right. Later on, Ben Thompson sold out and left town, and the Bull's Head reopened with a new owner and a new name.

I had every intention of leaving the next day. I really didn't want to be around to see what ramifications the activities of the night before would bring, and my job was actually done. I'd been there to back Bill when the showdown came, and it had come and gone.

I dropped my star on Bill's desk the next morning.

"Riding out?" he asked.

"In a while," I told him. "So there's no need to wear this any more."

"I won't have a deputy," he told me, but there was no real concern in his voice.

"Slap a star on old Nat, just for show—or maybe Roy, the bartender at the Alamo—until you get somebody. With Coe gone, somebody'll step up for the job."

Looking at Bill, you would never know that the man had been half-mad with grief and anger the previous night. He seemed to be in complete control.

"Where're you off to?" he asked.

I shrugged. "Anywhere. Someplace quiet, where there's no gambling, and no shooting."

"And plenty of women, huh?" he asked.

I nodded, smiling slightly and said, "Yeah, that too."

He stood up and put out his hand, saying, "Thanks for being here, Clint."

I took his hand and said, "What do you think is going to happen now?"

He shrugged, saying, "The town council will probably use this as an excuse to dump me. They've been looking for one long enough."

"I've got a couple of ladies to say good-bye to, and then I'll be on my way."

"Take care of that big horse, huh?"

"We look after each other. *You* take care, Bill," I said. Then, staring him straight in the eyes I added, "You know what I mean?"

"Yeah," he answered, "I know what you mean." But I knew he'd never get his eyes checked.

I left the office and tried to decide which lady to bid farewell first. I decided on Nell Virdon, since the Alamo was closer than the hotel.

The place was empty and Roy was mopping the top of the bar with a damp rag.

"Where's Nell, Roy?"

"In her room. You pullin' up stakes?" he asked.

"Soon as I can."

"Be careful."

"Yeah, you too."

I went up the steps and knocked on Nell's door.

"Who is it?" she called out.

"Clint."

"Come in."

I walked in with a smile on my face, ready for

a sweet send-off, but what I saw on her dresser stopped me short.

It was a flowered music box, and there was a small crack on the side, as if the man who bought it had dropped it.

It was the same box Coe was carrying when I waylaid him.

"I guess you came to say good-bye," Nell said, from behind her partition. She was getting dressed, having just gotten out of bed. "You should have let me know you were coming," she added, stepping out. "I wouldn't have even bothered getting dressed."

I walked to her dresser and picked up the music box.

"This is very pretty," I said, picking it up and turning it over in my hands.

"It's just a music box," she replied.

"I've seen one like it before," I said, watching her in the mirror.

She narrowed her eyes slightly, wondering what I was leading up to and said, "Oh, really?"

"Yeah, Phil Coe had it when I gave him a well-deserved beating. I'm afraid he stepped on it," I told her, running my finger along the edge. "He cracked it, just like this one."

I turned around to face her, holding the box in one hand.

"You know, I wondered why you were so nervous last night about me being up and around. I thought you were worried for me, but that wasn't it, was it? What did you do, offer to nurse me back to health, hoping that there would be some way you could keep me off my feet?"

"No, that wasn't it at all," she insisted. "I was really worried about you."

"Sure, Nell," I said. I dropped the music box to the

floor and crushed it with my heel. It let out one musical note, and we both listened as it faded out.

"Clint," she said, rushing to me and putting her hands on my arms, "you can't tell the marshal about Phil and me."

"Let me guess," I went on, as if she hadn't spoken. "Phil Coe owned the Alamo too, and you were just fronting for him. If Hickok had known that, he never would have spent so much time here."

"He'll kill me!" she cried out. "You can't tell him!"

I pushed her away from me and said, "Don't worry, I won't tell him—as long as you catch the next stage out of Abilene. If I hear that you stick so much as your nose back in this town, I'll tell Bill, and he'll take it from there."

"Clint—"

I walked to the door.

"Maybe you don't deserve killing," I told her, "but you sure as hell don't deserve the good-bye I was going to give you."

I walked out without another word. And then I headed over to the American House and found Allie working at the desk.

"Clint," she said quietly, smiling; then she must have realized why I was there, because the smile faded away.

"You're leaving," she said.

"I'm just going up to get my gear, Allie," I told her.

She put her hand on mine. "Let me come up with you?"

I shook my head slowly and smiled at her, taking her hand in mine. "No, little girl, then I might never leave. I've got one more errand to run, and then I'll be on my way."

Her eyes started to mist and she said, "You won't forget me, will you? I'll never forget you. It'll never be like it was with you."

"That's not true, Allie," I told her. "It'll be whatever you want it to be. Remember that. And no, I won't ever forget you."

I leaned over and kissed her lightly on her sweet-tasting mouth. I went upstairs to get my things, and when I came down she was gone from the desk.

I carried my gear with me over to the undertaker's and found the doctor there, drying his hands.

"Oh, Mr. Adams. I see you're no longer wearing a deputy's badge."

"I'm heading out, Doc. My job here is finished."

"It doesn't have to be that way, you know," he told me.

I looked at him and said, "Yes, it does."

He nodded and said, "I understand. What brings you over here?"

"I just wanted to make sure that Mike Williams's burial was being taken care of."

The undertaker spoke up: "The marshal is paying for it."

I nodded, and the Doc jumped in and said, "And well he should, since he killed the man."

"It was an accident," I pointed out.

"Be that as it may, he killed a policeman. I'm afraid the town council won't like that, any more than they will like the way he gunned down Phil Coe. Don't try to tell me that was an accident. I just took four bullets out of Coe's body."

I started to explain about that when I realized what he said.

"Four bullets?" I had fired once, and Bill had pumped two slugs into Coe's body. The only other shot had been the first one he fired, which I thought had missed everything completely.

"Yes, four. Odd, too," he said, frowning, "there were only three entrance holes in the body, and one of the bullets was not a .32."

"Three of them were thirty-twos?" I asked.

"That's right."

It was hard to believe, but apparently Bill's first bullet had struck Coe in *exactly the same place mine had*. There was no way of telling which bullet hit first, but they both went in the same hole! There was no other explanation.

Had it been a lucky shot, one fired by pure instinct, or had the problem with his eyes been a hoax? No, it couldn't have been.

Bill had no reason to lie to me about his eyes, and certainly no reason to shoot Mike Williams on purpose. No, the only explanation had to be that Bill fired his first shot on pure instinct, and it had gone straight and true, right into Phil Coe's chest, either right before mine, or right after it.

It was too bad we didn't know which bullet had hit first. That might have told me who was faster, Bill or myself. I thought I had fired a split-second after him, but the shots had been so close there was no way of being sure.

And maybe it was better that way.

Epilogue

All of that took place in October 1871.

In December I read an article in the papers that said Wild Bill Hickok was no longer marshal of Abilene, and that many of the gambling houses in that town had closed down. Reading between the lines, it was obvious that the town council had decided that they could do without Bill Hickok, and they could also do without the gamblers who had set up shop there for three years or more.

Abilene would no longer be the booming town it once was, but it would be a quiet town, a town with no trouble, and without a "killer" like Bill Hickok as marshal.

Bill had done his job, and now they didn't need him anymore, except as a scapegoat.

After that, I was never able to pick up a newspaper again without the fear that I'd find an article about the death of Wild Bill Hickok. I still haven't found such a story and I hope I never do.

Author's Note

This book is a novel based on fact. Certain incidents that happened, and certain people who did exist were used as the basis for this story.

The following people were in fact in Abilene in 1871, while Wild Bill Hickok was marshal of that town:

Phil Coe and *Ben Thompson* were partners in a saloon and gambling hall called the Bull's Head. Hickok did in fact order them to alter the picture of a bull with an exaggerated male organ which hung over the entrance outside the saloon, and when they refused he had some painters do it while he stood by with a shotgun. Ben Thompson and his family were injured in the manner described.

Frank and *Jesse James* did in fact enter into an agreement with Marshal Hickok whereby each party would leave the other alone.

John Wesley Hardin, who did shoot a man for snoring and then fled from town, was one of the most notorious figures of the West. The confrontation between Hickok and Hardin also did in fact occur and, as described in Hardin's own words, the young killer claims to have faced down the great Hickok. History cannot confirm or deny his account, but both men did go into the Alamo afterward and did form certain attachments to each other—which did not stop Hardin from leaving after the shooting.

Mike Williams, a friend of Hickok's, was hired as a policeman by the town council.

Tom Carson was an obscure man about whom little is known except that he was a deputy at that time. There is no indication, however, that Carson even worked for Phil Coe. Hickok did administer a beating to the man, but perhaps not for the reasons described here.

The Alamo Saloon also existed at this time and was Bill Hickok's favorite hangout. There is no indication, however, that Phil Coe had any connection with the place.

The incident in front of the Alamo described at the end of the book did occur, and it is true that during it Bill Hickok shot and killed both Phil Coe and, by accident, Mike Williams. It is also a historical fact that at this time in his life Hickok's eyesight was failing.

Of course, we cannot know for certain whether Clint Adams—or anyone remotely resembling The Gunsmith—was anywhere near Abilene at this time. But, although Mike Williams and Tom Carson are the only deputies named, history does state that Bill

Hickok had "two or three" deputies serving under him in Abilene.

J. R. ROBERTS

SERIES

An all new series of adult westerns, following the wild and lusty adventures of Clint Adams, the Gunsmith!

☐	30856-2	THE GUNSMITH #1: MACKLIN'S WOMEN $2.25
☐	30857-0	THE GUNSMITH #2: THE CHINESE GUNMEN $2.25
☐	30858-9	THE GUNSMITH #3: THE WOMAN HUNT $2.25
☐	30859-7	THE GUNSMITH #4: THE GUNS OF ABILENE $2.25
☐	30860-0	THE GUNSMITH #5: THREE GUNS FOR GLORY $2.25
☐	30861-9	THE GUNSMITH #6: LEADTOWN $2.25
☐	30862-7	THE GUNSMITH #7: THE LONGHORN WAR $2.25
☐	30863-5	THE GUNSMITH #8: QUANAH'S REVENGE $2.25
☐	30864-3	THE GUNSMITH #9: HEAVYWEIGHT GUN $2.25
☐	30865-1	THE GUNSMITH #10: NEW ORLEANS FIRE $2.25

Available wherever paperbacks are sold or use this coupon.

 ◖ ACE CHARTER BOOKS
   P.O. Box 400, Kirkwood, N.Y. 13795

Please send me the titles checked above. I enclose $_____.
Include $1.00 per copy for postage and handling. Send check or
money order only. New York State residents please add sales tax.

NAME_____

ADDRESS_____

CITY_____STATE_____ ZIP_____

Winners of the SPUR and WESTERN HERITAGE AWARD

Awarded annually by the Western Writers of America, the Golden Spur is the most prestigious prize a Western novel, or author, can attain.

☐ 29743-9	GOLD IN CALIFORNIA Tod Hunter Ballard	$1.95	
☐ 30267-X	THE GREAT HORSE RACE Fred Grove	$2.25	
☐ 47083-1	THE LAST DAYS OF WOLF GARNETT Clifton Adams	$2.25
☐ 47493-4	LAWMAN Lee Leighton	$2.25	
☐ 55124-6	MY BROTHER JOHN Herbert Purdum	$2.25	
☐ 82137-5	THE TRAIL TO OGALLALA Benjamin Capps	$2.25	
☐ 85904-6	THE VALDEZ HORSES Lee Hoffman	$2.25	

Available wherever paperbacks are sold or use this coupon.

ACE CHARTER BOOKS
P.O. Box 400, Kirkwood, N.Y. 13795

Please send me the titles checked above. I enclose $_____.
Include $1.00 per copy for postage and handling. Send check or money order only. New York State residents please add sales tax.

NAME_____

ADDRESS_____

CITY_____STATE_____ZIP_____

A–2